THE SWEET SWEET FRUIT

BY

DAVID W. JOHNS II

ISBN: 978-1-7372005-2-9

Contents

Start of Log. 1

Day 7 - Bowviolet Space Shuttle
- 358 hours until Earth Landing...1

Part 1 - Hilola Island...5

Day 8 - Bowviolet Space Shuttle
- 344 hours until Earth Landing.. 11

Part 2 - Departure... 12

Day 8 - Bowviolet Space Shuttle
- 332 hours until Earth Landing.. 14

Part 3 - Paradise Parks and Resort 15

Part 4 - Cobalt Quarters 22

Part 5 - Orientation - 1 of 2... 29

Day 10 - Bowviolet Space Shuttle
- 302 hours until Earth Landing.. 40

Part 5 - Orientation - 2 of 2... 41

Part 6 - Le Grande De La Reese... 50

Day - 13 - Bowviolet Space Shuttle
- 234 hours until Earth Landing.. 61

Part 7 - Eve's Apple... 63

Part 8 - Curse of the 7,000 Dollar Limoncello 71

Day - 15 - Bowviolet Space Shuttle
- 181 hours until Earth Landing.. 90

Part 9 - Royal Weight.. 91

Day - 15 - Bowviolet Space Shuttle
- 177 hours until Earth Landing.. 99

Part 10 - HOLLOW..100

Part 11 - Living in the palace...112

Part 12 - Dying in the palace...125

Day - 19 - Bowviolet Space Shuttle
- 184 hours until Earth Landing..129

Part 13 - Bad Omens..130

Day - 21- Bowviolet Space Shuttle
- 155 hours until Earth Landing.......................................137

Part 14 - Pure...138

Day - 28 - Bowviolet Space Shuttle
- 90 hours until Earth Landing...145

Day - 30 - Bowviolet Space Shuttle
- 42 hours until Earth Landing...147

Part 15 - Hilola + Kalbar 4 Ever....................................148

The Bitter Realities, as told by Princess Hilola 161

Part 16 - Dark & Sweet..165

Day - 31 - Bowviolet Space Shuttle
- 21 hours until Earth Landing...171

Part 17 - The Garden 173

Part 18 - The Graduation 177

Day - 31 - Bowviolet Space Shuttle
- 9 hours until Earth Landing...181

Part 19 - Escape from Paradise Parks & Resort 182

Day - 32? - Bowviolet Space Shuttle
- Day 1? on Earth...193

DAY 7 - BOWVIOLET SPACE SHUTTLE - 358 HOURS UNTIL EARTH LANDING

"Why is it so damn cold?"

Rebecca wanted one moment to herself. Just one moment where she was free to think without catering to her great grandfather's every whim and complaint. It was like this the entire trip. She stepped out of her lounge chamber and strolled down the white hallway, activating the motion-sensored ultraviolet fluorescents along the way. She walked out into the observation deck and there he was, four feet from the glass, huddled underneath a grey wool blanket. From behind, he looked like a decorative space rock. In fact, her great grandfather and a space rock were a lot alike.

Great Grandfather Space Rock slowly extended his leathery hand and pointed out into the starry darkness.

"You see that star? That one there. That's *my* star."

His tiny wrinkled face slowly managed a smile.

Rebecca ran her fingers through her shaggy blue bob and sighed.

"Where's the remote?" She asked. Her great grandfather didn't respond. Rebecca scanned the room; she checked in between the cushions of the furniture, checked inside the ottoman, and she rummaged through the storage cupboards. After a moment she found the remote, a small circular disc blending in perfectly with the cup coasters, and activated heat mode in his direction. The grey wool fiber blanket brightened a few shades and eventually turned a stark white.

"Dope." He purred, snuggling into the blanket.

"Do you need to go to the bathroom?" Rebecca asked.

"Where's Monclair?" Either he didn't hear her or he chose not to answer. Rebecca shrugged.

"She decided not to come. We aren't on the best of terms right now."

"Oh?"

"Let's say the only reason I'm allowed to even borrow the shuttle is because she loves you so much." Rebecca left it at that, hoping he'd drop the topic. He did.

Rebecca sat on the nearby sofa and studied Kelley Immerson Dodge, her maternal great grandfather. The last person she knew who was actually born on Earth. In 96 hours, he'd turn 90, which was quite the feat for people of his generation. His only wish was to be returned to Earth to celebrate his birthday in peace. No one else in the family could be bothered with such a silly request, and Rebecca's girlfriend…possible ex-girlfriend…owned her own shuttle, so naturally, this fell onto her shoulders. Plus Rebecca could use the time away. The trappings of her daily routine were beginning to feel suffocating.

"Rebecca." Kelley called.

"Yes, granddad?"

There was silence. Rebecca rolled her eyes, and got up to stand behind him.

"You called, granddad?"

More silence. Kelley slowly extended out his hand from under the blanket and patted on the ground beside him. Reluctantly, Rebecca crouched and sat beside her great grandfather. Together, they stared through the glass out into space.

"Do you ever get tired of looking at the stars?" Kelley asked, inquisitively. "I suppose you live among them so you rarely look at them at all anymore."

Rebecca looked at Kelley then back into space.

"It's not that I tire of them. I just don't feel anything when I see them." She paused, thinking. "What I feel is so much more important to me than what I see."

"Thatagirl." Kelley patted Rebecca's knee. "Great answer. You're very right. What you feel is more important than what you see. Never lose that faith in what you feel."

A small smile spread across Rebecca's face as she glided back into the moment and focused on the tiny blue and white swirled orb they were traveling towards.

"So why go back to Earth?" Rebecca asked.

Kelley was silent. He was silent when he didn't want to talk, or wanted to change the subject. His old age warranted that, and everyone took it as a sign of his fleeting memory and control of his own mind. Everyone except Rebecca. She just found it rude.

"How old are you now, Rebecca?"

"Oh, you want to talk now?" She asked sharply, half joking, before she could catch herself. Kelley chuckled. "I'm 20 years old. 20 Earth years, I should say. Why?"

"…Hm."

He shuffled and rummaged under his blanket, through his blue cotton robes. Rebecca pretended to seem uninterested by tracing a pattern in the floor with her finger, but she was curious.

The rummaging stopped and he gingerly pulled out a small dark object from beneath the folds of his clothes. He positioned himself slightly in Rebecca's direction and she, now at full attention, leaned in closer. He opened his hand and revealed an onyx black orb. Intrigue came over Rebecca as she studied it's grooves and rough texture. She motioned to his palm, silently asking to grab it.

"Be delicate." Kelley whispered with a hush of importance that she'd never before heard from him.

Using her fingertips, she grasped the object and caressed it. It was slightly familiar, yet foreign too. The roughness, the hollow fragility of it. She lifted it to her nose to smell, and something clicked.

"I remember this!" She said, more to herself than her great grandfather. "When I was very little, you let me hold this. It wasn't as dark as it is now, but I remember the smell. It's the hint of citrus. This…" She smelled it again. "…this is an orange?"

"Close. A lemon." He smiled.

"A lemon." She agreed, smelling it a third time. She closed her eyes and let the faded dark remnant scent of the dried lemon fill her nostrils. "And this one came from an actual Earth tree, right?"

"I was there when it was picked." Kelley nodded. "The lemon was given to me when I was your age."

She returned it to his hand and studied it, entranced, as he rolled it around his fingers. Rebecca watched him in concern.

"Why did you bring this out, granddad?"

He looked at her and when he smiled, his bulbous nose squished slightly upwards. His weather-beat skin was riddled with liver spots and the thin white strands of hair he still maintained were combed to the side, but there was a boyish charm to his smile that was almost disarming.

"I've decided I'm going to tell you a story," he said, "and whether you believe it or not is entirely up to you."

Rebecca stared into Kelley's face, nodding. "Ok."

"But first," Kelley put his index finger into the air. "a bathroom break."

Rebecca rolled her eyes and smiled.

Part 1 - Hilola Island

Long ago, there was a family who lived on a large island, Island Hilola, by the name of The Hunamas. Their family owned trees that produced the largest, brightest, most plump supernatural lemons the Earth had ever seen. They were the size of cantaloupe melons and grew in abundance year round. Of all their characteristics, the most unusual thing about the lemons was that they bore no seeds, so they could not be reproduced or duplicated. This distinction set them apart from other lemon farmers and in turn, they made the family very wealthy. So wealthy that they eventually were able to buy the entire island. They offered an ultimatum to the other natives on the island: either flee their homes or agree to a life of servitude under the family's ruling. Some left, others stayed. Together, they built HUNAM Corporations, and continued to export their lemons while creating lemon derived products. They sold toothpastes, house cleaners, perfumes, air fresheners, and of course, their very own patented brand of lemonade.

In 1965, the Hunama family underwent a massive rebranding and transformed Hilola Island into *Paradise Parks and Resort*, a theme park and hospitality resort catering to middle class families and the wealthy 1% alike. The resort was an immediate success and in no time the entire world was saving it's spare change to make Hilola Island their next vacation getaway.

It was my 20th birthday. I should've been carefree and beaming with happiness, not sleep deprived and harboring a large ball of nerves in the pit of my stomach. Yes, it was my birthday but I wasn't thinking of birthday candles and presents. All I could think of was the letter that would appear and change my life.

"You have to eat something, Kelley." My father yelled from the kitchen. The breakfast he'd made for me had gotten cold. I thought about heating it up, just as a way to show my appreciation, but the truth was I couldn't bear to eat. Not until I got the answers I needed.

I pushed my curly copper-brown hair off my forehead and shielded my eyes from the rising Texas sun. I hadn't been outside for more than 30 minutes, but my fawny skin was now dewey with sweat and threatening ruby undertones, signaling early stages of sunburn. One last glance at the horizon before picking up the newspaper and heading back inside. It had been a grueling four month process to get to this point: a $100 admission fee (non-refundable of course); two short essays, a $25 transcript fee from my high school; an online questionnaire; and an intense 45 minute phone interview at seven in the morning. Everything that could've been done had been done. Now, sprawled out on my mother's vintage loveseat in the living room, there was nothing to do but wait.

"Has the mailman stopped by yet?" I asked my father as he wiggled into his rubber boots at the front door before making his way to his award winning garden. Three years in a row now, my father, a self-taught botanist, had won a local landscaping award Brownfield Texas had put together and our backyard was the talk of the town every summer. He was pretty good at it, my dad. It was the only hobby that stuck after his mental breakdown. My mother's passing affected everyone differently. We all had our coping mechanisms.

"Not yet," he said with a sigh as he grabbed his gloves. I sulked further into the couch cushion.

"It'll come," he assured me. "In the meantime, look who I found in my glove."

I sat up, slightly more alert, and peered over. Dad opened his hand slightly and shook the opening of his gardening glove over it. Out dropped a small cherry red bug that righted itself and began to crawl about Dad's fingers. Its long spiny legs inched like a spider's onto the glove. I got up and walked over for a closer look.

"That's a milkweed assassin." I said as I examined it.

"Very good," my father exclaimed, turning his hand and extending his finger in his best effort to keep the moving bug from falling to the floor.

"But it's far too early for them to be emerging from the dirt." I was perplexed.

"Yes some of them are early, some are late, but they're all welcomed nonetheless. I'm going to put it in the roses. I thought it would cheer you up."

"Dad, now isn't the time for bugs," I groaned, before throwing myself back on the couch, dramatically.

My dad chuckled a bit and bounded over towards the backdoor. "It'll come."

And it did. Later that afternoon as I was getting some chores done, I heard the clunky commotions of a truck pull up. I quickly wiped the soap suds onto my shirt and raced through the living room and out the front door.

The mailwoman, an elderly lady with curly grey hair sticking out of the bottom of her safari hat, gave me a wave and a smile before stuffing a small stack of newspapers and envelopes into our mailbox and driving over to the next house. Within moments my dad and I stood over the kitchen table, together, looking down at the letter addressed to me, Mr. Kelley Immerson Dodge from HUNAM Corporations.

"Whatever's in there, Kelley…" My dad rested his hand on my shoulder and I immediately smelled the roses and pecan wood mulch from the garden. It was such a bittersweet smell.

"Whatever that letter says," he continued. "I want you to know I'm so proud of you. Finally, you followed through with something."

"Gee, thanks." I said half-heartedly.

"That came out wrong. I mean to say I've never seen you so dedicated."

It only stung a little because it was the truth. I barely managed to graduate high school and the only thing I had to show for my on-again-off-again relationship with community college was increasing debt. I could barely keep a job for longer than a year and the next job was just like the last. I hadn't applied myself in life and I was terminally undecided in everything.

Except this. I wanted this more than anything.

I picked up the envelope and broke the enclosing seal. The air seemed to have fled from the entire house as I removed and unfolded the letter.

"Read it out loud." My dad said somewhere nearby.

I cleared my throat and focused on the words.

"Mr. Kelley Dodge… First and foremost, we'd like to thank you for applying to Paradise Parks and Resort. With over a thousand applications every year, we strive for only the best. We are proud to say that this includes you. Yes, you have officially been accepted into the Paradise Parks and Resort College Internship Program with the very special opportunity to stay on as a regular member. Founder and CEO of HUNAM Corp. once said 'In giving everything one can, only then is one able to receive. In losing one's self, only then can one be truly found. In embracing fear, one can be free from it.' We hope you find yourself here with us, Mr. Dodge. Welcome to the island."

I could hear my dad's boisterous cheers behind me, but it was a muffled noise that sounded very far away. Time slowed like it does in the movies when someone gets shell-shocked. It was all suddenly very real. As my mind slowly started to process what was happening, I couldn't help but allow a smile to spread across my face. I was finally free from Brownsfield, and about to see so much of the world I'd only seen online. My whole life was changing.

I found my way deep into my father's arms. His chest heaving and holding back sobbing chokes that mirrored my own.

"I knew you could do it. I'm so proud of you. Your mother would be so proud of you, Kelley." He said in deep breaths. We stood there in silence, embracing, a couple more moments before the delivery guy with the take out we'd ordered minutes ago rang the doorbell.

Four days later, I stood in the airport with my grandmother and my luggage. Dad had taken off work to drive me into Austin to my grandmother's but had to get back the night before my morning departure time. We said our "See you later"s and without much more lingering, he was back on the road. Standing at my terminal, I tried not to pull on the hem of my new oxford blue blazer, but my nerves refused to leave well enough alone. The sun had not yet risen and I would be taking the first nonstop flight out to Hilola Island.

My grandmother, a stout barrel of a woman, retrieved a lint roller from her gigantic purse and began furiously rolling it across the crotch of my khaki pants.

"Grandma!" I shooed her, mortified.

She then proceeded to stand on her tiptoes to simultaneously straighten my tie and fuss over my hair.

"I really wish your mother had moved to Austin with me. Brownsfield…What did you learn in Brownsfield?" She tossed the word 'Brownsfield' past her lips as if her tastebuds didn't agree with it.

"Well, I think…," I began.

"Don't sass me," she interrupted. "The outside world isn't like your hometown. It's large and dangerous and new and amazing. Just remember who you are and what you believe in."

She pulled out a nice sized wad of cash and attempted to shove it in my pants pocket.

"Grandma!" I hissed.

"This is for food." She continued, unfazed. "Real food. Buy whatever you want with your first paycheck, but you'll buy protein, starch, and a vegetable with my money. Understand?"

I tucked the money safely deep into one of the shoes in my backpack. "Yes ma'am."

The gate attendant announced the boarding of the nonstop flight to Hilola Island. A few families eagerly gathered and waited to board the plane.

"Ok. Ok. Ok." She whispered as she dusted off my coat shoulders and stepped back. Her mouth was beginning to tremble as she covered it with her fingers, looking up at me with soft pride. Her eyes glazed over and a smile escaped past her fingers. "I know your father made you do something stupid like make you promise to come back, but I want you to live your life. Enjoy this. Find your place in this world. He'll be just fine."

The trembling gave way to full on shaking. "You're in for the ride of your life, Kelley." She embraced me hard.

The gate attendant made the second call for boarding.

"We love you. Do well. Be good." She whispered into me, and without another word she turned away and headed for the exit. I waited a moment in case she looked back. She never did. Like mother, like son I suppose.

Day 8 - Bowviolet Space Shuttle - 344 hours until Earth Landing

"Grandma sounded like a badass." Rebecca sat down in the mostly empty dining hall for breakfast with her great grandfather and Quon, the Bowviolet's astrographer and Rebecca's grade school friend. She peeked over his shoulder at a card game he was playing with another crew member. The cards were seemingly blank, but when pressed, they revealed their holographic number and symbol. He noticed her over his shoulder and with a reduction of pressure, the cards erased themselves and were blank again. Rebecca scoffed.

"Touchy."

Quan laughed, "Focus on your breakfast, Captain."

Today it was oat milk poured over a mixture of dried grains, nuts, and fruit. Real healthy shit. Rebecca poured an extra scoop of raw sugar into her bowl before she began eating. Her great grandfather sat across from her over a cup of coffee, deep in thought.

"She was." He smiled and looked up at her. "All the women in our family possess that quality."

Sheepish, Rebecca blushed and turned her attention to her bowl of food. "So shall we continue?"

Kelley thought for a moment. "Yes. Now the volcano, it was quite-"

"Whoa!" Rebecca shakes her head. "You've gone too far. Back up to getting to the island."

"Oh. Yes. Of course."

PART 2 - DEPARTURE

I swung my backpack over my shoulder, picked up my duffel, and headed through the gate onto the plane. After locating my seat I buckled in and took a couple deep breaths as the other passengers filed in past me. My face felt hot and I could feel the tears welling up. I felt silly for feeling so emotional and pulled the blind down on the window before sinking back. After a moment, the flight attendant, a slender middle aged woman with a giant purple flower in her hair, came by with a tray of drinks.

"Hello there. Can I offer you a drink?" She asked sweetly. I looked up at her, managed a half-smile, and shook my head, declining. The lady set her tray down on the armrest and kneeled down in the aisle.

"Interning at Hilola Island?"

"What gave me away?"

"You and maybe five other people on the plane have the same nervous look on your faces. I remember when I first interned."

Nearly lost in the memory, she smiled.

"It's natural to be nervous about the unknown, but I know a part of you is also excited. If you aren't excited, you wouldn't be here. If you aren't excited, you *shouldn't* be here."

There was some sense of warning in that last part, but I let it go, trying not to dwell. She had a point. This is what I wanted.

She looked swiftly over her shoulder, then leaned closer. "Are you over the age of 21?," she whispered.

"I just turned 20 this month," I whispered back, though I had no idea why we were whispering.

"Close enough," she said, handing me a large cocktail glass. She stood and straightened her skirt with her free hand.

"From now on, when someone asks if you're over 21, just say yes." She secured her tray and applied her artificial smile. "You'll do fine. Enjoy the flight!" She walked on to the seats in front of him and began to coo over a toddler who was yelling at the top of his lungs.

I leaned back and examined the cocktail. It was a pale murky yellow with purple flower petals mixed in. Could they be from the same flower the flight attendants wore? I pulled the straw towards my lips and took a sip. It was maybe the best, freshest lemonade I'd ever tasted. It was ice cold, but calmed my nerves with a soothing warm sensation. I drained the glass. Afterwards, I placed the empty glass on the tray beside me and reclined. No longer able to hear the obnoxious toddler, I settled into the slight numbness of whatever the hell was in that drink, which I didn't mind at all. After a moment I lifted the blind of my window and was greeted by the vibrant gold and pink clouds as they swirled in the sunrise.

DAY 8 - BOWVIOLET SPACE SHUTTLE - 332 HOURS UNTIL EARTH LANDING

Rebecca tucked her great grandfather into his sleeping chamber and checked his vitals on the bedside screen before leaving. She walked to the Command Center, where she held the position of captain of the shuttle. She pressed a little button in the shape of a sound wave.

"Samuel, status reports on the shuttle's current vitals, please."

"Vitals exceptional." A metallic male voice from the speakers.

She rechecked the routing system. They were on schedule. When she was fully satisfied, she sat in the Commanding Chair and reclined. It smelled like Monclair. Aldehyde and hot honey. Rebecca inhaled deeply and held it in a moment before letting it go. The farther away she got, the more petty and meaningless their fight had seemed. She wished Monclair were here. She wished she could contact her, if only to hear her voice, but that would be an unreasonable waste of resource energy. Not to mention she wouldn't know what to say, so she pushed her from her thoughts.

Rebecca clicked a button on the chair and the metal shades gave way to present a wide scope view of Earth shifting ever so slightly in space. She found herself looking past the orbital debris, at the white swirls of earth, and she tried to picture clouds. She'd never seen natural ones in real life. She wondered if her great grandfather saw them in his sleep. She wondered if great grandfather Kelley was going to Earth to die.

PART 3 - PARADISE PARKS AND RESORT

I jolted awake to find passengers passing me to exit the plane. I rubbed my eyes a little and squinted out the window. I saw nothing but the runway and in the distance, an ocean dock. Absolutely nothing else. I steadily collected my bags and joined the line of departing passengers.

The sun beamed as I stepped onto the tarmac and I was greeted by a small band of island locals. This beautiful girl stepped towards me after greeting the woman in front of me. The girl was tall and curvy with the tiniest banana leaf skirt and what appeared to be a strapless bikini top made entirely of peach colored roses. Her soft brown skin shimmered in the sun and her raven hair was pulled into a loose ponytail.

"Welcome to Hilola Island." She said warmly. Cheeks reddening, I bowed slightly and made a mental note to pronounce it as she did in her native tongue: E-LOO-LAH.

She presented me with a flower crown consisting of pink hibiscus buds and peach roses, similar to the one she wore, all woven together by a lush green vine that bore bright yellow berries. She placed the crown of my head and adjusted the vine slightly until it fit snug across my forehead. I thanked her again, more audibly this time, and continued down past the group of islanders playing what looked like handmade drums and flutes and a bunch of children going wild over mascot Papayago, a large square colorful cartoon styled tiki carving that danced around them. It even high-fived me as I walked past.

Papayago, the only mascot at Paradise Parks and Resort, was essentially a man in a full body tiki mask with a pair of arms and legs covered in tattoos growing out of it. Wide enough to where only his arms were visible and long enough to show a bit of bare knee, Papayago was complete with two large dark slits for eyes, an extremely wide toothy smile, and a bushel of large banana leaves sprouting at the top of his head.

The next thing I noticed was how the cloudless blue skies almost became one with the blue ocean waters. I then saw a small striking red boat with a large orange sail in the distance and a massive white and gold yacht pulling up to the dock. I took my place in the forming line that led up to this impressively big yacht; there I waited to board the ship.

After a while I started taking stock of a few people, people who looked around my age, being ushered out of line and grouped aside by a skinny older man with a large black mustache and questionably short khaki shorts. He seemed to be asking them questions and depending on their answers, he'd motion to the growing group of people behind him. I caught myself fidgeting and tried to seem casual as the man approached and eyed me suspiciously.

"Good afternoon young man, and welcome to Hilola Island," he said in fabricated cheerfulness. Also he pronounced it HE-LOLA island. "May I please see your ticket to Paradise Parks?"

A slight grin appeared on his face, and I knew that he knew I didn't have a ticket.

"I'm with them over there aren't I?" I half-joked with a shrug and began walking over to the group. Anything to cut the conversation short before thigh highs got a chance to further humiliate me. He even managed to sneak a small scowl from underneath his mustache as I passed by.

When I finally made my way over to the group, I could clearly see it was four girls and three other guys. This ratio changed as more followed behind me. We were gathered around one another, fiddling with phones that had no signals, kicking loose gravel from the tarmac, and avoiding each other's curious glances.

"You with the internship?" I asked aloud, boldly, to no one in particular but looking about the entire group. No one spoke for a beat, but then a guy sitting on his suitcase towards the side of the group spoke.

"Duh."

His response lacked any malice, and his smirk was one of gratitude for breaking the awkwardness, I figured. In an effort to make a friend, or an acquaintance at least, I walked over to the boy, fashioned my duffle bag into a seat, and sat beside him. The guy must've been tall because his knees were parallel to his shoulders as he sat there, scrunched. As the uncomfortable silence began to grow again, I just wished I hadn't sat so close to this guy. Now I felt obligated to make conversation.

Before I could even think of anything to say, the boy pulled a pink e-cig from his basketball shorts. I watched, captivated, as he tapped a gold button on the side and put the mouthpiece on his lips. The tip of the wand glowed blue as he inhaled and almost immediately after his first drag, the thick velvety smell of weed hung in the air. A few girls scoffed and moved away while mostly everyone else did their best to ignore it. I was just happy to finally have a topic of conversation. I leaned over in the guy's direction, slightly.

"How'd you get that through the airport?" I asked, genuinely curious. The guy said nothing. He just looked over at me and grinned. At least, I assumed he was looking at me. His eyes were completely hidden underneath dark brown unruly hair that mushroomed the entire upper half of his head and stopped just past the bridge of his nose. His grin was wide and curled mischievously at the ends. It made me squirm, but I managed to return a smile and tried to shift my focus on a plum colored beetle that shuffled by.

Well, it stomped more than shuffled. This beetle pushed passed loose gravel or climbed over it entirely, stopping every once and awhile to enjoy the patches of lush green grass that broke through the concrete. Tiny oasis in a barren desert.

Two heavy drags later, the guy spoke.

"So what are you running from?"

I thought for a moment. "I'm not running from anything. My hometown is small and it's crowded. Looking for a change, I guess."

The guy nodded. "That's fair. Still running, but fair."

My brow furrowed, still trained on the beetle. "What about you? What are you running from?"

"My old man, of course." He took another long drag. "Promised him I'd apply to law school after the internship. He's making me quit my band." He went silent again and it was so deafening it caught Kelley's full attention. The guy seemed lost somewhere, then he stuck the wand in between his lips and shrugged. "This is my last attempt at procrastination. My last hurrah, if you will. Just another smoke break."

I nodded.

"This place is paradise on Earth." A round girl with curly red hair and an early onset of sunburn nearby snapped at him. She was carrying a backpack covered with images of Papayago making funny faces and stuffed Papayago plushie sticking out of one of the compartments. "Not just another way to run away from your responsibilities. You should respect the happiness Paradise Parks brings to people."

The ends of his mouth curled wickedly into a smile as he peered from below his hair up at her. "Yea? Well we'll see how much happiness it brings you after nine hours of food prep or starting and stopping the same ride 700 times every day." He was so aggressive in the way he spoke, everyone was now listening to him. "Don't get it twisted, princess. They're putting us to work."

Shaken by this exchange, the girl rolled her eyes and turned away. I knew the guy was right, but from what he'd seen on TV and in magazines, the place truly did look like paradise. How bad could it be?

Just then the man in high shorts dragged himself up to the group. He eyed us all before speaking. His fabricated cheerfulness from before, now an authentic monotone loathing.

"Like I said, welcome to Hilola Island. My name is Mark. I will be your Intern Advisor for the duration of your stay. We will be boarding the service boat…" He half-heartedly gestured to the red boat with the large orange sail now pulling up on the dock."…and once we arrive at Paradise Parks and Resort you will fill out your paperwork, get your job title, and receive your keys to your housing units. Any questions?" He glared at the group, threatening them to have any questions.

"Need I remind you that Paradise Parks and Resort is a child safe, DRUG FREE…" he leaned aside, putting his full attention on the only guy smoking, "…environmentally friendly island. Starting now use of drugs and underage drinking will result in immediate termination. The tampering, stealing, breaking or corrupting of any and all Paradise Parks and Resort property will result in immediate termination. You will be fired, removed, and banned from Hilola Island for up to five years."

He looked amongst our collectively terrified expressions and smiled, satisfied.

"But you all look like a great group," he said. "I'm sure we won't have any problems. Follow me, please."

He turned and headed to the dock. Everyone gathered their things and followed suit. As the red boat floated against the dock, it looked a lot smaller than it did miles out in the ocean. One by one, people began boarding. Mark walked straight towards the shaggy haired boy and confiscated his e-cig.

"Starting now!" he repeated, allowing him to board. The captain turned the wheel and we set sail out into the blue ocean.

I didn't mind the trip, or the limited space to sit or stand, and the old captain who occasionally shouted curse words at either the ocean or one of the kids in his way. I didn't even mind the boat smelling like dead fish laid out in the afternoon sun. It reminded me of my fishing trips with my father and grandfather as a kid. The boat cut swiftly through the currents and a constant saltwater breeze felt good against my forehead. In the distance, Paradise Parks came into clearer view.

The island, a singular mountain ascending from the ocean, was covered in lush green jungle and adorned with clouds rolling down its sides. My heart was pounding as I leaned out of the boat for a better view. There was an undeniable buzz amongst the interns; we were all lively and in good spirits as the boat bound closer to the parks. We began to make out the tons of people on the beach, sprawled about the white sands. Once we reached the reefs we passed a group of young surfers gathered together, lounging about on their paddleboards. A kitesurfer no one saw coming nearly grazed the bow of the boat and sent the captain into a cursing frenzy, which some of us found hilarious. Soon after, I noticed a few girls on the boat pulling compact mirrors out to primp their hair or apply more lipstick. Then a guy nearest him became fixated on the direction his bangs were falling. By the time they reached the shore, everyone no longer looked like they'd just arrived off a jet lagging 8-hour flight, but instead like they were about to audition for the hottest new television teen drama. I wiped the corners of my mouth and eyes, just in case.

As the boat docked, everyone was ushered off and let loose amongst the thousands of other interns arriving. There were people from all over the world and everyone seemed to be young and vibrant and attractive. It was as if I'd just entered the coolest beach party ever, and I was overdressed. As I wiped the sweat from my brow, I tried my hardest not to gaze as a group of girls in extravagantly colorful sari dresses passed by. Instead, I focused on following Mark down the sandy trail and up to a large warehouse where everyone was formed into an extremely long line that headed inside.

"You all will be here until you've gone through registration!" Mark yelled amongst the chatter. We were herded besides several other interns and their intern advisors and it became evident that the high shorts were a uniform. Many of them spoke in languages I had never heard, but the expression of disdain and self-loathing was uniform as well. "I will see you all bright and early tomorrow for orientation!" Mark nodded and joined the other advisors as they began to walk off down a separate trail. I stood there silently amongst the roaring chatter of friends and strangers meeting for the first time. I eavesdropped on two girls in front of me giggling and talking way too fast about some boy they'd met on the boat ride over and figured they wouldn't want me interjecting to make introductions. I then glanced behind me, accidently locking eyes with a sun kissed girl with wavy blonde hair. She was wearing a white see-thru shirt with a blue bikini top. Her matching bikini bottoms peeked out from under white cutoff denim shorts and her legs…

"Hello. Up here." Her cool voice shattered the trance I hadn't realized I was in.

"Hello. I'm sorry." I chose not to hide how intensely red I was getting as a personal form of punishment to myself.

"Charlene. Portland, Maine." She held out her hand.

"Kelley. Brownsfield, Texas." I smiled, taking her hand in mine and squeezing it softly.

"I didn't mean to stare." I said honestly. "I just wish I had worn board shorts instead of this stuffy suit."

She smiled as she eyed him up and down. "Oh, well, yea. I'd much rather be on the beach than in this line."

"Right?" I agreed.

"And you look great, by the way…" Charlene smiled warmly, "…but you should probably move up or you're gonna get cut."

She pointed over my shoulder and I spun around to find that the line had moved up exponentially. I nodded before catching up and filling the three person gap.

We moved up a few more yards closer to the warehouse. It was a giant steel building that had been taken over by the vines and exotic flowers. Small rust patches could be seen the closer you got.

When I passed the entrance, I was met by a woman at a desk kindly asking for my identification. As I handed her my ID card, she assured me that I'd receive it back after registration and with a smile I was ushered forward. I then proceeded to be photographed, fingerprinted, measured, and weighted. They examined my eyes, my throat, my teeth, my blood pressure, and my hair. I was at some point given a pen and signed off on several legal forms mentioning my likeness, my health, any allergies I may have or develop, and what would happen if I were injured, killed and/or eaten.

"Just old precautions." They said, smiling.

Three hours later I walked down a flight of stairs and found a lady sitting next to the exit door. For a brief moment I thought of ignoring her and just sprinting for it, but really…at the very least, the thought put a smile on my face.

"You've made it!" She said cheerfully. She pulled an envelope from a file cabinet and placed it on her desk.

"Name please."

"Kelley Immerson Dodge" I said, for the 50th time today.

The lady pulled my ID card from the envelope and confirmed my name and face.

"Here you go!" She handed me my ID and the envelope. "Enclosed is your job title, a map, your housing unit and house key- don't lose that -, and a brief history of Paradise Parks and Resort. Ok! Enjoy your day! Don't forget orientation at 5:00am in the morning!" She waved as I walked out the door and into the sun, now positioned to set.

I was still in hearing distance when Charlene came down the stairs to an identically cheerful "You've made it!"

PART 4 - COBALT QUARTERS

Kicking at rocks and dead bamboo stalks, I set off down the given trail for my housing unit when I came across a group of young boys playing on the path. They were carrying bamboo sticks and yelling at one another. None of them looked over the age of twelve years old, with bright eyes and their chubby cheeks full of chewing gum. As I cautiously approached, pretending to pass by uninterested, one boy stepped forward. He was shorter than most of his friends and thin, with a crazy jagged haircut and he was covered in dirt and bruises.

"Hey!" He yelled with such authority it made me stop in my tracks. "Funny looking man. What are you doing here?"

Slightly hesitant and confused as to what was going on, I cleared my throat and spoke up. "Um, I live here now? I'm headed to Cobalt Quarters."

"He says he lives here now," he announced confidently to the boys behind him. A few boys scoffed and crossed their arms. "I am Yung Phoenix Kalumaj. Descendant of the Spirit That Crawls. 7th incarnation of the Maji Tribe Emperor. Conqueror of the Reef of Death."

Another boy closely behind Yung Phoenix Kalumaj inhaled deeply through his nostrils and hacked up a large glob of spit, which he flung onto the dirt beside him. His hard gaze burning a hole into my chest the entire time.

"What is your name?"

"Just Kelley." I muttered, blankly.

"I live here, Just Kelley," Kalumaj said. "you are passing through, yes?"

"Yes." I quickly responded, and attempted to walk past the boys before one of them held out their hand.

"Yes." Kalumaj nodded his head slowly, agreeing. "You will sacrifice to appease the Gods, yes?" Kalumaj asked, smirking with a glint of something fiendish in his eyes.

"What do you want?" I asked.

"Gold," he demanded, sticking out his dirty little hand.

"I don't have any gold!" I sneered, widening my chest and raising to my full height over the boys. I was tired, my feet hurt, and it was far too hot to play games for much longer.

The boys looked up at me for a moment, startled, then looked at one another.

"…do you have candy?" One of them asked, his stern demeanor cracking just a bit. Kalumaj shot the boy a fiery glare for breaking rank and attempting negotiations.

Of course I knew I was being shaken down by a bunch of island kids, but I was on their turf so I had to play by their rules. After a sigh, I reached into my pocket and pulled out an American five dollar bill and watched as the boys' eyes widened with amazement.

"Will a fiver make this all…" I waved the bill in the air, and the boys' heads moved with it, like hungry puppies. "…be over with?"

I slowly placed the bill in Kalumaj's hand and walked past.

"Just Kelley, friend of the Maji Tribe!" I heard Kalumaj yell some distance behind me before they went back to their game. I couldn't help but smile and shake my head. If a gang of preteen boys were the most of my worries in the jungle, I could live to accept that.

The map they'd given me was easy enough to read, though the jungle brush didn't make it without difficulty. Once I reached the clearing of the housing units, the raw undeveloped jungle trail gave way to well groomed hedges and clean modern living quarters. Standing beside the massive fountain at the entrance, I could gaze down upon the cliff sides and see bungalow style apartments below tennis courts below a large infinity pool. The crystal clear waters mirrored the bright blue sky and there wasn't a cloud in sight; it felt like heaven, almost. It was the humidity that I couldn't handle. By the time I had reached Cobalt Quarters, a small apartment complex colored in blue and white detailing, my shirt was dripping with sweat. I pulled the envelope out of my bag and fished through it until I pulled out a large bronze key. It had '#14206' scratched into the back of it. I found building 14, then found the apartment door with '206' on it in dodgy black lettering. This had to be it.

I adjusted the bag hanging off my shoulder before inserting the key and turning the knob.

I entered the room and walked instantly into someone's home; there was a large Brazilian flag on the wall of the dining room, various papers and shoes and cartoon figurines cluttered about the floor, and the only thing stronger than the smell of dirty dishes from the kitchen was the pulsating thump of electronic music coming from one of the rooms. I checked my key again. I checked the numbers on the door. There must've been a mistake. There had to have been. This couldn't have been it.

"¡Se você pegá-lo, ele nunca vai se curar, idiota!" A boy yelled as he exited the room where the music was coming from. He was tall, stick-figure skinny, and had a head of thick curly brown hair with sun bleached ends. Eyes wide, he looked alarmed to see me. "Oh, hello."

"¿É que bastardo Edvin?" Another voice from inside the bedroom.

"Não, é um novo companheiro de quarto, acho." He eyed me suspiciously, as my discomfort levels rose.

"¡Momentos de diversão!" The boy yelled as he walked out of the room. Almost immediately I realized that the two boys were identical twins. Only difference was the other boy had long brown dreadlocks and a tiny tattoo of a heart below his left collarbone. He stuck out his hand. "Hello, I am Fausto, São Sebastião, Brazil. This is my brother, César."

"Kelley, Brownsfield, Texas." I shook his hand.

The boys gave me a slightly perplexed look.

"Texas?" César asked. He mimicked my accent, pronouncing it TECH-SIS. "Where is this…Texas?"

"Umm." I froze there for a minute. "Texas. It's, um, in America. USA. Umm…"

The twins stared blankly at me, then Fausto jumped and clapped his hands together.

"¡Texas! ¿Lembre-se de todos aqueles filmes de cowboy que uma grande mãe assistiu? Haveria sempre algum homem branco, alto para ir.."

Fausto then stuck his foot out on its heel, tipped his imaginary hat and in perfect southern English said "…Howdy Partner."

"Oh! Texas!" César's face lit up and he began to mimic shooting pistols in the air while Fausto pretended to ride a bull while swinging one arm in the air wildly. I sighed, unamused.

"Yes. Texas, yes. Ok, so did I make a mistake? Where is housing for new interns?" I caught myself speaking loud and slow, which made me feel even more stereotypically American.

"Mistake? No, I think not. You have a key, we have extra beds. Welcome home!" César shrugged. "There is a bed there, down the hall, and another over there, in the room across from ours."

Just then the front door swung open with a bang and a boy towered in with arms full of grocery bags. He was the tallest of all of us, and built like the guys on the football team I tried to avoid in high school. His black hair was cut into a fade and his dark brown skin was drenched from the humidity.

"I got dinners and all your silly little junk foods for the week." He spoke to the twins in a crisp British accent. He glanced at me just for a moment, then walked the bags into the kitchen. "Don't ask for change because I spent it all. You'll get over it."

He came out of the kitchen drinking from a large bottle of water. I licked my lips a little, realizing just how thirsty I was. My eyes followed the water bottle as he put it down on the counter and stood in front of me while the twins rummaged through the bags.

"You can't stay here, mate." He shot at me, towering from a couple feet away.

Completely thrown by the boy's comment, I snapped back into focus and looked up at him. "….I'm sorry?"

"Look, you're not the first boy César has tried to move in here to play house. I'm not having it. Scoot on, yeah?" He leaned back against the wall, his demeanor casual yet firm.

"That was only two times! You think you are so smart. He is the new roommate and you are no fun!" César spat from inside the kitchen. "¡Ele acha que ele é tão inteligente!"

"I actually just met César and …um…"

"Fausto." Fausto called out, annoyed.

"…and Fausto like, a second ago. He's right. I am new here." I explained, trying to keep it together. It was all so much to take in, and I couldn't think straight enough to not get kicked out.

The boy nodded his head and surveyed me. I must've looked pitiful. "Yeah? Show me your papers then."

I handed him my envelope and the boy pulled out a white paper and looked it over.

"Well there you are!" He said matter-of-factly as he handed back the envelope. "Welcome home."

"Thanks?" I responded, visibly relieved. I then made a beeline to the kitchen where I grabbed a plastic cup and filled it from the tap. The cool water washed over my tongue and I noticed something there. A refreshing tartness and a familiar crisp bite. Then came the smell.

"Is there lemon in the tap water??" I asked, astonished, impressed, and to be frank, rather rejuvenated.

"Yeah, kinda. So the HUNAM Corporation plants are near the housing apartments and the zest from the cooked lemons makes its way into the water supply…or so we've been told." The boy shrugged. "It's harmless to drink on occasion but don't make it a habit, yeah? The acidity from the lemons eats away at your teeth and the walls of your mouth."

I nodded, taking another sip.

"Completely sorry about the interrogation, mate. I swear, I didn't become a total beast until I started living here with 3 other roommates. Fresh start, yeah?" He extended his hand. "Keith, Bristol, United Kingdom."

I shook his hand and introduced myself. "So exactly how long have you guys been living here? Are you interns?"

"Yea. Most internationals have the option of getting here three months earlier than you lot just to get used to American customs. It's Day 1 for you, just in time for the opening season." Keith walked off to join the twins in stuffing their faces.

I turned to the faucet and refilled my cup, masking my astonishment. I was upset about walking into a previously established house —a house with its own history. Its own rules and regulations. I couldn't help but feel like a guest. How long was that gonna last?

"Well," I said with a long sigh. "I'm going to get settled. Take a nap. See you later guys." I stood there in the kitchen and waited for a response. There wasn't one. The guys stood over the dining table and ate and talked as if I didn't exist. After a moment I just picked up my bags and made my way past them to the room near the kitchen.

After making the twin bed and hanging my clothes in the closet, I finally looked around the room. It was clean. My roommate kept all his things close to his bed and in his space. I changed into a pair of sweat shorts and a lightweight tee and laid across the bed. I stared up at the ceiling and tried not to think about how far away from home I was, all by myself. I tried not to think about how discomfort and sadness were slowly wrapping themselves around my chest and neck like a scarf. No, I didn't think of those things. It's too soon to be homesick. I closed my eyes and let the sound of my breathing —in and out, in and out— enter the otherwise silent room.

I woke up in pitch darkness. Groggy and thirsty. I lifted myself up from the bed and opened the door. The disorientation only lasted a moment as I slowly walked down the hallway. As I turned the corner and entered the living room, I saw a short Asian guy sitting cross-legged on the couch, only illuminated by the ever changing colors of the television. He fumbled for the remote and froze like a deer in headlights when he saw me.

"I'm sorry. Is this too loud?" He said in a low hush.

"No, not at all. You're fine." I walked over and shook his hand before sitting down. "Kelley, Brownsfield, Texas."

"Paulie, Glendale, California."

"Nice. So you just got here today?"

"Yup. To be completely honest I didn't expect there to be people already living here. It's kind of…kind of…"

"Kind of fucked up." I nodded. Paulie nervously chuckled.

"Exactly." He nodded. "What you said."

We sat in silence watching TV. Some old game show from the 70s was on. A man in a shaggy bowl cut hairdo tried to mime things to a woman in a paisley mini dress, while the host continuously patted his afro and made jokes about the contestants. In the end, he won. A girl in a hula skirt and heavy eyeliner came out and presented him with a cardboard cutout surfboard as the walls behind them separated to reveal a tropical island setting. The woman in the mini dress fainted when the host announced that they'd won an all-expenses paid vacation to Paradise Parks and Resort. The irony of it all.

"I'm far too nervous to fall asleep." Paulie mumbled, unprompted.

I looked over and through the light of the blaring TV, I saw a look of hard concentration on his face and the nervous tapping of his foot. He watched TV but mentally you could tell he was thousands of miles away. Something inside me really sympathized with him.

"Hey, I'm nervous too. But this may be the coolest, most amazing thing I've ever done. We've made it this far. Might as well enjoy it, right?" I smiled and Paulie nodded, returning the smallest of smiles . I patted him on the shoulder and headed for the kitchen to get myself a cup of water, then I walked myself back to bed.

That next day started at a moonlit 4:00am. I was getting dressed when I noticed the roommate I hadn't met yet snoring soundly in a shroud of darkness on the other side of the room. I quietly grabbed my dress shoes and tie before leaving, where I joined Paulie quietly chewing a danish wrapped in a napkin near the front door. We nodded at one another and headed outside. The new interns were to dress business casual and meet at a bus stop outside of the apartment complex. There, we'd board a number of white school busses and be shuttled further into the island. We all settled in and were off. Elephant ear leaves the size of beach towels swiped at the sides of the bus as we made our way down the narrow road. Most of the interns either stared blankly out the window, headphones on, or had their heads back and eyes closed. I listened to a group of girls nearby quietly converse in a language I didn't understand until their small talk was overtaken by the scenery outside my window. The dense lush jungle fell away almost suddenly to open-air evergreen fields colliding with the rose gold explosions of sunrise breaking through the clouds. A couple miles ahead, we approached towering stone hedges oddly placed on their most narrowed ends, but they also seemed to have blossomed from the tall grass themselves. Everyone was pretty awake and alert by this time, as there were several oohs and ahhs in the bus. A couple people lowered their passenger seat windows for a better look and within minutes the smell of wet grass, and lemon zest wafted through the bus. The pink and golden hues of the sun highlighted the carvings of faces and animals etched into the monoliths. Eyes glued to the standing stones as they passed by, I wished we could have stopped and checked those out a bit more, but I had to remind myself I wasn't on vacation. A few miles later, we arrived at a large warehouse. It was very similar to the warehouse we first encountered on the island, but this one was miles from the jungle. It had no vines climbing its walls or moss occupying its corners. Instead, the glass windows gleamed and the golden accents that snaked around the beams and frames really shined. Outside in the well decorated entrance grounds stood two men and two women, dressed similarly in white and tan suits. They smiled as the interns exited the bus.

"Good morning, darlings." The shorter woman beamed. "Follow us. We have so much to do and so little time in the day!"

We followed them into the lobby of what looked like an old school, where we were broken into groups then ushered into classrooms.

In every classroom there was a television, notepads, and a giant pitcher of lemonade on the table in front of the room. Before the class began the instructor asked if anyone would like a cup of lemonade; everyone lined up for a drink. It was so fresh and perfectly sweet. It was too good not to pass up. Then we were taught, interactive lecture style, about the local plants, local wildlife, the park, and the volcano near the northern portion of the island.

"Is it active?" A dark haired boy asked from the back of the room.

"Yes and no," The instructor replied. "The volcano, Kalbar we call him, is completely dry for six months. That is because the magma is let out underneath the island. When the magma builds, however, it breaks the crust of the base of Kalbar and fills him all the way to the top."

"Why is the volcano a he?" A tiny girl asked near the window.

"Because he's a king." The girl beside her interjected, politely. "I came here years ago, and as the story is told, King Kalbar falls in love with wild Princess Hilola and promises to tame her before their wedding. He tries with all his might to calm and control her, but no matter what he does, nothing changes her nature. Consumed by his anger and love for her, he becomes a volcano on the morning of their wedding. He roars and threatens to destroy the entire island. Princess Hilola sees her people in dread and despair and gives herself to King Kalbar, calming his temper." She finished in a low hush. The room was so quiet you could hear the ocean waves crash outside in the distance.

"That's romantic." A square-headed boy seated in front of me said aloud.

"That's sad." The tiny girl who asked the question whispered, looking down at her notepad.

"Sometimes romance can be sad." The instructor smiled. "But we're getting ahead of ourselves." A timer went off and we were directed to another classroom down the hall.

We learned about the beaches, the sections of the resort, and finally learned about where we'd all be working.

"For instance, Edgar." The instructor spoke to a blonde kid as she pointed to the cobalt blue roller coaster on the map. "You will be operating The Wave, the fastest roller coaster created by any theme park in the world. Isabelle?" She then gave full attention to a tall athletic looking girl in the front chewing gum. Well, *was* chewing gum. The moment she heard her name, she gulped and swallowed it by accident. My eyes widened. "You will be keeping a vigilant eye as a lifeguard here at Rocco Beach." She pointed to the northeastern side of the island on the map of the island displayed on the board.

"And Kelley," she said in what sounded like a slow boom, "you will be working at Le Grande De La Reese. Our most prestigious resort here at Paradise Parks. Where the wealthy elite go to unwind. You are a very lucky boy. I just hope you are a quick study." She chimed with a wink before turning back towards the board and continuing her lesson. I didn't hear much of anything afterwards, honestly. My mind was reeling after what I'd just heard. Me? Working at the most expensive resort, surrounded by the richest people? Oh my God, the celebrities! The closest I'd ever been to a movie star was when I helped a friend of mine cater for a film cast and crew while they were shooting a show for a week in Brownsfield. The actress was our age, and was known for a blockbuster film she had starred in the year before. She was polite, but stayed within her circle much while she was there and didn't interact with any of us townies. The show they were filming never got picked up and so ended my brief brush with stardom. But my new job would place me amongst powerful, highly regarded individuals. Individuals who were the masters at their craft and were paid handsomely for their talents. Them, and their golden egg trust fund children. Most importantly, they would now rely on me. I felt the red hot glares of my classmates upon my body. I adjusted my posture and pretended to listen to the lecture unfazed, but inside, I knew this was a big deal. I knew I had received the lottery win of intern jobs at Paradise Parks. I put my head down and copied notes but as the sun rose outside the classroom window, so did the joy spread across my face.

Nearly 15 hours and nearly 12 different classrooms later, the interns were corralled into a large cafeteria for dinner. I couldn't decide whether I was starving or exhausted more, but nonetheless I shuffled into line and picked up a tray of what looked like a shepherd's pie, a side of whole snap pea pods, and a slice of pineapple upsidedown cake. We were given a cup and had the option of soda, water, or lemonade. Few chose the lemonade.

Everyone pretty much stayed close within the groups they were placed into that morning and socialized with one another in the cafeteria. Gazing around from my table I found Paulie across the hall, staring solemnly at his tray, surrounded by a group of rowdy boys much bigger than him. I called his name a few times, waving, but he never looked up. He only picked at his food and moped quietly to himself. I figured it was best to not disturb him and instead struck up a conversation with the dark haired boy who sat near me in class. Bentley was his name, from Cheyenne, Colorado. He got the position of the new roller coaster conductor at the park.

"Mr. Fancy Pants!" Bentley teased with a smile as he chewed his snap peas. "Who'd you screw to get that job? Come on, you can tell me. I can keep a secret." His grin was devilish.

"If it makes you feel any better, you can say you were responsible for making a million girls scream this summer." I teased back.

"I like the way you think." Bentley nodded before sipping from his cup.

It took me a few minutes before I noticed a few men in maintenance uniforms quietly setting up a large projector screen at the front of the cafeteria. They worked diligently and efficiently, and once the projector screen was raised, they moved on to the wiring. More interns started to notice them too, and before they were done, the entire cafeteria was buzzing. All eyes were glued to the front.

"Now, what's going on here?" Bentley asked, more towards himself, because no one at the table answered.

After the men were done and a large projector system now stood before them, they silently walked out of the cafeteria. Moments later four tall men in black business suits entered and stood militantly in front of the screen with their hands behind their backs, silently looking over the cafeteria with expressionless faces. Then a woman walked in and time stood completely still. I couldn't even hear the hum of the air conditioning; there was complete silence.

She was drop dead beautiful. Clad in red heels, fishnet stockings, and a skin tight khaki colored pencil skirt. The dark floral silk blouse she wore seemed to wave and flutter as she walked and her curly black hair bounced with the giant red amaryllis staying perfectly still set behind her ear. I made a mental note to congratulate myself later for remembering that type of flower taught in class. I had a knack for those types of things. Very much my father's son.

She stood in front of (who were now obviously) her security guards and smiled warmly at the crowd before speaking.

"Good evening everyone. My name is Regina Hunama. Many years ago my great grandfather, Ricardo Hunama, built this beautiful park and opened our home to the world. Today I stand before you and make the same gesture. Here at Paradise Parks and Resort we strive for a luxury experience that is unlike anywhere else." Her tone was warm and inviting. "We pride ourselves on our work ethic, our dedication, and our service. I would be out there doing every job myself if I could, but I can't. I need a team of young talented people who I can trust to do the job for me…" She paused, and looked into everyone's face with a sympathetic smile. "…and I know this is that team. So this week I want you to embrace this island as your home, treat your new careers with love and respect, and above all…make me proud."

Regina curtsied slightly and the room gave her a hearty applause. Some even cheered and whistled. We are completely enamored.

Regina laughed and hunched her shoulders forward in a Marilyn Monroe-esque fashion. "Now I'd love to grab a bite and get to know you all better but my work never ends. So, I'll leave you with the live stream of the summer's opening ceremony here in the cafe! Thank you all once again and remember, if you ever need anything, you can contact me through your counselors. You guys are the best!" She was met with more applause and cheers. She put one hand over her heart, and waved with the other as she exited the cafeteria, the three suited men following closely behind. The entire room was electric.

"She's so damn cool!" Isabelle gushed to everyone's agreement at the table.

"Well I, for one, am not getting any sleep tonight! Did you see her body?" Bentley yelled as he high-fived me and a few other boys at the table behind him who laughed at his statement.

"She not only manages Paradise Park but she runs all HUNAM Corporations." I overheard a girl say.

"Not to mention she's the Hilola lemon heiress. She's friggin' ROYALTY!" The girl beside her shrieked. They kind of lost all communication and motor skills afterwards and turned into one big tangle of starstruck fangirls.

I was just as charmed by her as everyone else was, but I'd be a fool if I didn't admit, at least to myself, that between her well memorized speech and the four bodyguards, something about the whole thing felt a tad off.

Just then the screen clicked on and the image of Kalbar the volcano appeared, towering before a purple twilight sky. Red smoke billowed from the mouth in ribbons and cascaded down the sides. There were a number of small helicopters zipping by and circulating the massive volcano. The camera panned further out and you could see the large crowd that had gathered at the base of it. Suddenly red fireworks shot out from the mouth of the volcano and the smoke turned a bright red. People in the crowd shrieked. Even a few people in the cafeteria jumped. Then, you could start to see people emerge from the jungle around the volcano. The women were wearing these beautiful skirts and tops made of dark blue leaves and adorned heavily with these bright white shells that practically glowed in the dark and rattled when they danced and stomped. They wore them on their ankles, wrists, and around their necks and waists. The men wore loincloths made of the same blue leaf, the shells on their ankles and wrists, and what appeared to be white ocean coral fashioned around their heads to make a crown. All decorated and gorgeous, dozens of these people slowly made their way into public view and started to spiral up the volcano in a ceremonial dance to the beat of rapid drums and tribal chanting. As they began to reach the top, the foggy smoke of the volcano began to lighten in color from red to a faint pink all the way to a stark white. So white, it was as if there were white lights within the smoke itself. Suddenly two hands became visible from INSIDE the very middle of the volcano. Nearly half of the cafeteria gasped. Some people were even pointing. The hands swirled and danced about the surface of the smoke, then sank back down out of sight. I craned my neck to catch a better view of the screen. As the dancers reached the top, they suddenly froze, hands up and panting in unison. Again fireworks shot from the mouth of the volcano and as the shiney white embers fell down from the sky, a girl rose from the center of the volcano. She rose until it seemed she was standing on smoke alone. Her long curly black hair blew gently in the high winds. Her brown skin was illuminated by the white smoke and her outfit, which consisted of tons of white straw fashioned into a dress and large white leaves encrusted with gold for a bodice. She wore a dozen gold bangles on each arm and a silver head dress encrusted with glowing jewels and stones of different colors. The camera shot a close up of her face as she stared all around her with big honey brown eyes and full pouty pink lips. She looked as if she was seeing the world for the first time as she spun around taking in the view from every angle. She even mouthed a "wow" as she peered on in astonishment and curiosity. She rubbed a stray curl back from her face, locked eyes with the camera, and then she did something that made my heart flutter and took my breath away so unexpectedly; she smiled the biggest, brightest, most perfect smile I'd ever seen. I almost instantly blushed, but felt a sense of relief when I looked about the cafeteria and noticed that we were all falling in love with her at the same time. Bentley beside me, clutching his chest and moaning in false agony, which made everyone nearby laugh. I even noticed Paulie in the crowd, mouth agape and eyes glued to the screen.

"Princess Hilola," whispered Isabelle behind Kelley. "In the awakening of the summer season, she emerges from the volcano in her wedding dress."

Princess Hilola lifted her arms and swayed and spun to the rhythmic beat. She practically glided across the surface of the volcano.

"How does she do that?" I asked aloud, to anyone and everyone.

"It's smoke and mirrors. Literally," answered a guy with a buzzcut at the table behind me. "I'm guessing the smoke is being pumped in and she's on a glass surface. I bet the volcano isn't even real."

"Of course the volcano is real," shot a girl from the next table over.

"Well how do you wire an active volcano with fireworks, lighting equipment, and a dancefloor, genius?" He shot back. "All I'm saying is that this is just like any show back home in Las Vegas. This whole island, it's one big show."

"You're 100 percent right. I know that." Isabelle spoke in an attempt to extinguish the heated conversation. "But my family came here 10 years ago and saw this exact same show, and Princess Hilola looks like the same girl in the show from back then. Like, identical. My father? He visited once when he was 15 and again at 22. He says it's the same girl…I legit just gave myself goosebumps." She held her arm out for those nearby to examine. "There's no way that can be the same young girl from over 30 years ago…right?"

"Umm…prosthetics, you know. Face contorting through makeup and stuff. Drag queens and online makeup artists do that stuff all the time." The buzzcut guy said, though not as confidently as his first statement.

"Wait so is it real or-?"

"Oh my God!" Groaned someone from the back of the room. "Can you all just shut up and watch the screen?"

Feeling second-hand scolded, I turned and focused my attention back to the monitor as Princess Hilola was crowd surfing down the volcano from the arms of the dancers until she reached the bottom and was placed on a bed of white petals that were previously laid out for her.

The crowd applauded wildly, pushing slightly against the barricades separating them. She was stunning and vibrant, looking around at everything as if she were enchanted by it, all while never shying away from the camera flashes and cries of people clamoring for her. I didn't consider myself gullible; I figured she must have been an actress on contract for the next three to five years perhaps. Surely she hadn't been Princess Hilola for the past *30* years. I figured her age to be 25 at max. Isabella's father saw another actress. No way it could have been her. Absolutely not.

After the ceremony was done, we were put back on the buses home. I sat down and after more people filed in I noticed Paulie.

"Hey, man. Where are you stationed on the island?" I asked as he approached.

"Nature Control," he muttered, being shuffled forward.

"Wow. What does that mean?" I asked, earnestly .

"It means I'm fucked." He shot back, and without another word was pushed past somewhere far behind me.

"Oh. Cool." I nodded awkwardly moreso to myself.

"Do you know what's out there?!" I heard him yell from somewhere deep in the back of the bus amidst everyone's loud chatting.

The bus eventually started and it wasn't until we entered the pitch blackness of the jungle did I realize how exhausted I was.

As Paulie and I entered our apartment that night, we realized there was a tall lanky guy with unruly blonde hair ruffling through the kitchen drawers, while muttering furiously to himself in an unrecognizable language. Paulie looked at me cautiously as we made small steps towards the living room. We didn't get far before the boy's head shot up from behind a cupboard door. His eyes were wide and laser focused on us.

"Hello. Nice to meet you." He muttered in a thick European accent as he rushed over and aggressively shook our hands. "Hello, very nice to meet you both. I am Edvin, of Örebro, Sweden. Which one of you ate my ramen?" He asked with a smile.

Both Paulie and I just stood there, wide-eyed. Paulie shook his head.

"I, um, it wasn't…wasn't me. I had pizza last night." Paulie stammered. Edvin simply nodded and locked his wide eyes on me.

"I didn't eat at all last night." I muttered flatly.

"Ok!" Edvin yelled. "That means that no one here ate my ramen. Who ate it? We don't know! Alla vill spela spel." He threw his hands in the air and they remained there in mid shrug as he circled the room. "I spent my last filthy little five American dollars on this country's sad excuse for a noodle and I come home to find MY dinner taken…by ghosts!" He bellowed, filling the air with his voice. I had never seen such a spectacle; he was circling the kitchen island, opening cupboards and staring at their contents before laughing and slamming them shut. "But it's ok! It is as they say, A-Ok." He smiled wildly. "I will not starve tonight. I am going to eat from this kitchen until I am stuffed like the Christmas goose. And no one will stop me." His eyes darted threateningly to Fausto and César, who'd come out from their rooms to see the commotion.

"All the power to you, bruv." Keith said from the sofa, which startled me as I had no clue he was there. "I'm sorry about the ramen. I didn't eat it!…" he held his hand up, cautiously, "but I'm sorry it happened. My grub is your grub, mate."

There was a moment of silence while Edvin looked each of us in the eye before walking over to the pantry and opening it. He stared at the shelves of newly bought dry goods for a good minute before snatching a large bag of mini chocolate chip cookies. There was an audible gasp from Fausto and he clasped his hands over his mouth. Edvin never took his menacing glare off Fausto as he opened the bag and slowly pulled out one small cookie and put it in his mouth. Everyone was still as we watched Edvin chew that cookie. Every crack and crunch of his jaw sounded like an earthquake. Then, in what seemed like an act of utter maniacal possession, Edvin tilted his head back and turned the entire bag upside down over his open mouth. I'll never forget the sheer horror on Fausto's face as cookies fell from the bag and either landed in Edvin's mouth or on the floor. Cheeks completely stuffed with mini chocolate chip cookies, Edvin threw the bag behind him and glared at Fausto.

"¡DESGRAÇADO!" Fausto cracked and lunged at Edvin, knocking him down. They squirmed around in headlocks on the kitchen floor as César tried to break them up. Keith jumped from the living room sofa and began filming the fight on his smartphone.

"Give 'em the one twos, Fausto!" He chuckled, trying to get artistic with the phone camera angles. "Edvin, you just gonna take that, mate?"

I closed his eyes and took a deep breath. It had been a long day. Too long a day. This was all just…gratuitous.

"Night, Paulie." I said, patting Paulie's shoulder before making my way to the bedroom. I stepped over Edvin's writhing legs and managed to pick up one of the cookies that hadn't been squashed or stepped on.

"Five second rule." I mused to himself with a smile before shutting the bedroom door behind me.

Day 10 - Bowviolet Space Shuttle - 302 hours until Earth Landing

Rebecca sat cross-legged on the floor while her great grandfather sat on the couch. He was picking cashews out of a small container of mixed nuts and pieces of dried fruit and vegetables. Rebecca looked up at him, puzzled.

"What's ramen?" she asked him.

Kelley shrugged, eating his cashews. "It's a dried mound of pre-packaged noodles that comes with it's own pre-packaged seasoning.

"Sounds awful." Rebecca grimaced.

"It wasn't that bad." Kelley nodded in agreement. "The seasoning is riddled with sodium and the noodles could be fresher, but they were cheap…and pretty great when you were hungry and had no money."

"So you ate a lot of ramen before you invented the soul seed."

He chuckled, "Yes, I did. And I didn't necessarily *invent* the soul seed. I found ways to cultivate it and breed it with other plants. It was much later when I realized these plants didn't need oxygen to grow."

"You developed a group of crops that could grow in the soils of planets that had little to no oxygen, thus practically writing the manuscript of intergalactic agriculture and fortifying the human race's ability to survive on other planets. Granddad, do you fully understand how amazing you are?"

Kelley smiled. "We're jumping ahead. Now, where was I?"

Rebecca helped herself to the remaining dry mix and guided her great grandfather back towards his story.

I was in a deep sleep when the knock on the bedroom door came. I took a second to grasp my surroundings, then cleared my throat.

"Come in," I croaked.

The door cracked open and fluorescent kitchen light beamed in and around the still foreign faces of Paulie and César.

"Hey, house meeting. Real quick." Paulie murmured softly.

It was the night before their first official day and I was in no mood to sit up and listen to one of the guys bitch about a few marshmallows missing from their box of cereal.

"If this is about a candy bar or the dishes I'm going to be very pissed."

"You're gonna want to get outta bed for this, amigo." César called through the crack in the door, then they both left, leaving the door open. I sighed and thrashed about in my sheets for a minute before getting up and leaving the bedroom.

There on the kitchen table was a long wooden staff with what looked like wet dark brown gauze wrapped over one end. Beside the staff was what looked like a map of the park. Just then Fausto entered through the front door. He stood beside me and carefully turned the map over. On the other side revealed *another* map very similar to that of the main park, except everything was faded and barely legible. Everything but a route marked in black ink that isn't shown on the other side. It was bold and thick, as if the ink was poured on the map and never dried. Keith was hunched over it, tracing the trail with his finger without touching the ink itself. He traced the route which started just outside their housing complex, passing the main courtyard, through the jungle, and ending at the volcano.

"Talked to the girls next door," he said. "They have one too. I think we're all supposed to meet at the volcano."

"But why?" I asked, perplexed. My curiosity grew as I did my best to shake the drowsiness and study the map a bit harder, looking for any details we may have missed. It looked old and had creases as if it had been folded several times.

"It does not matter," Edvin was sitting on the couch going through his phone. He then stood up and joined them at the table. "We have to go. All of us. It's a test of strength. Everyone is going and if we stay, they'll never invite us to anything else and we'll be piss poor, socially. We'll be outcasts. You want to survive on this island? Get dressed." He turned and walked off to our bedroom without another word, leaving us stunned by this declaration.

"That was a little dark." Keith winced.

"He does have a certain way with words, doesn't he?" I added.

"Well, he's not wrong." Fausto shrugged. "¡Vamos!"

I walked into my room and put on a pair of khaki cargo shorts and a grey shirt. Edvin found a clean pair of denim jeans and slid on a sleeveless hoodie. My mind was racing. Where were we going? Who left the map? What was waiting for us at the volcano?

After everyone was dressed, Keith swiped the map, gave me the torch, and Paulie grabbed a few water bottles from the fridge and dropped them in his drawstring backpack. Outside, the night air was humid but cool with a slight breeze. Every star shown through the cloudless sky and the bright reflection of the moon illuminated everything in the deep dark blue. We didn't even need the torch or the map as they made our way towards the courtyard. Various birds and insects called loudly as we passed. I recognized two Reggiana birds flying from one tree to another, their long ribbon-like tail feathers trailing behind them. I tried to make out their signature rose color but it was impossible in the moonlit shade. Under Keith's guidance, we made a slight left towards a back alley in the opposite direction of the parks. Keith slowed for a moment, then came to a halt in a narrow gap in a 10 foot bamboo wall. We passed through the wall and found ourselves at the edge of the jungle.

"You are certain this is the entrance?" Edvin asked, peeking at the map over Keith's shoulder.

"Trust. There's no party I can't find. I've sniffed out raves using far more complicated directions," Keith replied, proudly.

"I can't do this. I'm not ready!" Paulie squealed. I could feel him shaking behind me and thought maybe he should've picked up a few weapons instead of water bottles.

César pulled a lighter from his pocket. "No worries, amigo." He tried to get a flame, but came up short.

Paulie shook his head. "No worries? You didn't attend the WildLife class I attended. You don't know about the things inhabiting this island!" Fausto snatched the lighter from César's fingers. "How bad could it be?"

He got a fire instantly and lit the top of the torch I was holding. It immediately grew into a pulsating blaze. The sudden illumination caused what looked like an entire wall of tiny once hidden critters to crawl and slither away from the shrub ridden entrance. The boys stood there in complete horror until Keith linked his arm with mine and we all slowly inched closer into the thick jungle.

We walked cautiously as we heard clicks and hums coming from above, following us as we moved forward. Whatever they were moved swiftly from branch to branch, making scratching and clawing sounds in the tree bark. I looked up to find a dozen pairs of glowing eyes looking down back at me. It was then I decided it was probably best not to look up anymore. Instead, I concentrated on my roommates.

"So your job, Paulie, is to be out here in the jungle?" I asked in a hush, throwing the question behind me.

"Unfortunately. As Nature Control, my job is to make sure the trails are safe for the guests and maintain overall cohabitable peace between civilization and the elements of nature." He proclaimed all in one breath as if he were reading his job description verbatim.

"So, what types of things were you speaking about?" Edvin asked, unable to hide his concern as we made our way deep into the jungle. Even as our torch burned fiercely in front of us, we were only able to see a few feet ahead. Every now and then Keith would stop completely and make a slight adjustment in our direction and we would follow, reluctantly.

"Oh, ok. Well, there are langur monkeys, parrot snakes, haplopelma lividum, tiger leeches, daddy longlegs…"

Fausto hissed. "¿Esperar o quê? What does haplo…?"

"Haplopelma lividum." César interjected.

"Obrigado. What does that mean?"

Paulie turned around and looked Fausto square in the eye. "Blue. Venomous. Tarantulas."

"¡Mãe de Deus!" César yelped and both twins looked to their feet as they walked on.

"Oh, did I mention the giant flamingo tigers?" Paulie spat, shaking his head.

"The flamingo tigers are just a myth!" came a shrill voice echoing from somewhere inside the jungle, making us all jump. Even Keith shuffled back and shielded his mouth with the map. We stood frozen in silence as we watched a girl hack through nearby bamboo with a giant machete. She pushed her sweat drenched hair out of her face and smiled politely before ushering a group of girls through the cutaway path.

"Flamingo tigers are named after the pink and purple hues of their fur. Their fur changes color based upon their diet, just like flamingos! They are thought to be extinct…" She stumbled through the portal and dusted herself off. "…if they ever existed at all."

She extended her hand out to Paulie. "Cassandra. Rosario, Argentina."

"Paulie-Paul, Glendale, California." Paulie stammered his intro, shaking her hand.

"Pleased to meet you, Paulie-Paul. Are you boys heading to the volcano?"

Before Paulie could speak, Keith stepped up. "On our way now. Are you and your lot doing the same?"

"We were and got turned around." Cassandra and the other girls side-eyed a tall brunette who pretended to focus on her map while simultaneously managing to avoid everyone's gaze. "We were hoping to tag along with you?"

"But of course, ladies." Edvin chimed in, his creeper smile visible in the dim firelight. "Me and my roommates, we're the type of company you want in this dark dangerous jungle."

The five of us stared at Edvin in disbelief before Keith spoke. "…Yeah. Let's carry on then." He stared down at his map under the torch light for a moment, then proceeded to walk through the jungle, now with a large group of 11 following closely behind.

"Flamingo tigers!" César whimpered, clinging on to a girl who was also now clinging on to him.

It wasn't long before we came across another group, then another much bigger group. By the time we reached a clearing halfway up the volcano, we were a good sized crowd. I wiped my forehead and looked out at the view of the jungle and at the ocean underneath the moonlight before pushing forward. We joined a group of boys up at the volcano's edge, which couldn't have been more than 10 yards wide, and cautiously peered over into the foggy abyss. Deep under the smoke, I could make out flashing lights and after a moment the steady vibrations of heavy bass music could be heard. Keith jumped in the air and hollered out over the jungle.

"The rage-hound hasn't lost his touch!" he yelled before hugging Fausto.

"Hey, there are stairs over here!" Someone nearby yelled and we all slowly made our way down the spiraling staircase inside the volcano.

"I told you the volcano was fake." One of the girls near me told her roommate. I studied the surroundings as I made my way down; It looked real. The rock was jagged and warm and there was a smell of sulfur, but I'd never seen the inside of a volcano before so I didn't exactly have a say in authenticity.

I reached the bottom and immediately stepped into what looked like a rave in a steam room. There were dozens of indistinguishable bodies wearing glow jewelry twisting and gyrating in the lights amongst the fog. The floor looked like dull glass but was rock solid, and it seemed to have a red glow coming from underneath. It was humid, but we were all already sweaty from the trek over. Paulie fished his inhaler out of his pocket, took a quick drag, and together we made our way through the crowd of dancers.

I squeezed my way to the front where the DJ drummed on a synth sample board in the middle of a small stage that looked like it was made from crystallized glass. Behind me there was a throne made of the large glass shards growing from the floor. Just as I was beginning to bounce to the rhythmic beat, I heard the shrill caw from above. I raised my head to look out of the mouth of the volcano just in time to see a massive reggiana bird fly past, it's blush colored feather illuminated by the lights of the party below. Suddenly I felt a hard shove into my right shoulder blade and before I could catch my footing I was hurling forward, my face meeting the clear quartz floor with a thud.

"My bad!," said a cheery male voice from above. I fought to maintain consciousness as a group of jewel adorned and henna tattooed feet walked past. I slowly pulled myself to my knees as the group that pushed past me stepped onto the stage and started dancing. There were two muscular statuesque guys and four long haired curvy girls twirling about and bouncing to the beat. The six of them were all stunningly attractive, but one of the girls I couldn't take my eyes off of. Her shimmering brown skin, full lips, and that smile. My eyes widened as she laughed and danced not ten feet away. That was Princess Hilola. She IS Princess Hilola!

She sat back in her throne as the two muscle-heads carried over a large golden hookah lamp. By now everyone there was either unabashedly gawking, or sneaking glances while pretending not to notice her. One of the girls in her entourage, a tall modelesque Asian girl with sleek straight carmine colored hair, handed her a goblet with a lemon wedge on the rim. Princess Hilola took a sip then threw her hair back out of her face, fully content. She glanced down at me and we briefly locked eyes. I looked off to the side as people started walking towards her. Everyone crowded the stage and started cheering and calling her name.

"Form a line!" One of her guys, the tall one with a curly blonde caesar haircut, barked and the people closest to him jumped back and sheepishly began to form a line. "Fucking savages. Every year."

Another one of her girls laughed. She was a tall dark skinned black girl with long thick legs and full curly chocolate brown hair that swayed as she chuckled. She continued to drink and dance beside Princess Hilola and her throne as people shuffled forward in line for phone selfies, shamelessly flirting, and gushing over her. She took it all in stride and even played along with a few of them, blowing thick white swirly clouds of hookah smoke into the face of a confident guy getting too close. After every meet she thanked them for coming and they were ushered off by the other muscular half of her bodyguard team. This guy was Middle Eastern with a chiseled jawline and disarming hazel eyes. He smoothed his jet black hair back to the nape of his next and forced the greeters ever so slightly over towards the bar and away from Princess Hilola. I was pretty sure he was the one that pushed me down.

"She's way prettier in person." Keith's voice came from beside me. Both Keith and Paulie were there, sipping straws out of onyx rock tiki cups. "Like, her looks could kill a man." He sighed.

I got up onto my feet and dusted myself off.

"Been making new friends I see." Keith grinned and pointed at my cheek. It was only then did I notice the hot sting as sweat entered the red slit above my cheekbone.

"What happened?" Paulie asked, genuinely concerned.

"Ah, it's nothing. I fell." I shrugged it off, wiping the floor off the front of my shirt.

"Sure you did. A painkiller, mate?" Keith handed me his tiki cup and I finished the drink in one large swig. "Right you are!" Keith cheered.

"Cheers…mate." I grinned as Keith playfully wrapped his arm around my neck. We then returned our gaze back to Princess Hilola. She was dancing on her throne while her friends entertained her. She laughed at something when she locked eyes with me again and her smile faded. I did my best to avert my gaze again but this time she casually motioned us over. Shocked, we pointed at ourselves in question.

Princess Hilola nodded.

As we stood before her, she sat high above us, hookah smoke billowing from her nostrils like smoke from a fire breathing dragon. Her girlfriends twirled and gyrated around us like sirens as the lights bounced off their shimmering skin and tight clothes. The corners of the Princess' mouth curled into a devious grin and at this close distance, she was terrifying.

"What are your names, boys?" She asked sweetly. Keith stepped up first, a sly drunken slack to his face.

"Name's Keith, Ruler of Bristol." he said, coolly, in a short bow.

"I'm Paulie. Paul. You can call me Paulie if you like. I'm from California. Glendale specifically. It's a small town. Mostly a community of senior citizens. And Armenian Americans. But mostly-"

Keith raised his hand and covered Paulie's lips with his fingers as he smiled up at Princess Hilola.

"Thank you, Keith." She nodded, winking at Paulie before setting her eyes on Kelley.

"And you." She studied my face. "I apologize on behalf of my staff." She eyed the dark haired boy a few steps away from her while he looked forward pretending not to listen.

I shrugged. "This? It's nothing. I'll be fine. I'm a big boy."

"Oh?" said one of Princess Hilola's girls from behind me. She was tall and slender with stardust freckles and thick platinum blonde hair. "Well, just how big a boy are you?" She began to pull up the bottom of his shirt from behind.

Princess Hilola hissed and the blonde immediately retreated back to the other two girls, who were snickering and grinding against one another nearby. Princess Hilola then took the lemon wedge of her goblet and turned her attention back on us. "How rude of me. I never got your name."

I cleared his throat. "Kelley, from Texas. Pleased to meet you."

"Pleasure." She smiled. "Rub the lemon on your cut. It's gonna hurt like hell, but it'll heal faster."

I graciously accepted the lemon wedge and followed her instructions. It stung, but I did my best not to wince.

"Texas, huh? Does that make you a cowboy?" Princess Hilola leaned back in her chair.

Between the balmy heat, the ever changing dance floor lights, and whatever liquor was in that black tiki cup, I figured my blushing was well hidden, but Princess Hilola's glare made me second guess this theory. I wasn't exactly the smoothest, but I knew girls, and I knew I was being teased. Both the blonde and Princess Hilola were pushing my buttons and I knew that. I had to play along and I had to be clever.

"Depends on what I'm riding."

Both Keith and Paulie whipped their heads over in my direction, astounded.

"Excuse you?" The blonde boy growled as both male guards towered over. The girls dancing next to Princess Hilola's throne burst into bashful laughter. Even Princess Hilola put a finger to her lips in an effort to keep composure. As she called off her dogs, he couldn't tell if she was blushing or it was a trick of the light.

"Well on THAT note, I want to thank the three of you personally for choosing to work here at Paradise Parks and Resort. Make your way to the bar and have a drink on the house. Hope to see you guys soon."

We were ushered towards the bar by the dark haired guy. "Sorry for…that." He playfully pressed his thumb against the cut below my eye before shoving us off, but my adrenaline was so high, I barely felt it.

"And the cowboy?" Princess Hilola called out to us over the dancefloor noise. "Make his drink a double."

PART 6 - LE GRANDE DE LA REESE

Early the next morning, I suppressed nausea and a dull headache while the bus made its way through the jungle and to what looked like an elaborate steel black archway standing 10 feet up in the air. We then entered two miles of lemon grove fields lush with plump yellow lemons and blossoming milky white flowers. That now familiar scent of wet moss and citrus filled my nose and made me forget about my hangover.

The shuttle bus drove up the dirt road to Le Grande De La Reese, a large triangular prism made of what looked like over a trillion clear glass shards set in a castle of white sand. It made me think of the photos I'd seen of the Taj Mahal only the way the sun rose and reflected off the mosaic glass made the building glimmer like raw precious stone. The closer I got, the more I was convinced that the glass shards were actually fallen stars, resting from a long night. That particular thought made me smile as we drove past the prism and stopped just in front of a dark green warehouse camouflaged by the jungle flora. My new resort coworkers and I got out of the bus, when two men in white suits opened the warehouse doors and frantically ushered us in.

"Hurry the hell up! You aren't on vacation!" hissed a short pale man with a brown 1950s style slick side part.

"Hurry before someone sees you!" hissed an equally short Asian man with a black slick pompadour.

They both shoved us all into the warehouse and shut the door behind them. The inside was a brightly lit space filled with dozens of aisles and compartments where at least a hundred people stood feverishly at work.

"This is called The Cocoon," the pale man said loud enough to be heard over all the commotion. "You will enter here everyday before work and go into hair, makeup, and receive your wardrobe for the day."

"You can only clock in the moment you're complete." The man with the shiny pompadour eyed us all, one by one, before clapping his hands twice. "Let's get you started!"

They then separated us into three perceived gender groups and guided us into different compartments across the room. The rest of the guys and I stripped down to our underwear and lined up one-by-one before entering cubicle style compartments. First, I found myself standing in front of a man that took my body measurements, then I was sent over to a barber station where a tall dark man with a face covered in tattoos sat me down and fastened a barber's gown around my neck.

"Ok young man, working at Le Grande you don't have many choices, but you do get to choose your hairstyle…out of these previously selected and pre approved hairstyles."

I looked up at the hair models on a poster hanging beside the mirror.

A No. 1 - A slick and polished side-part with the ends curled and waved towards the ears.

A No. 2 - A thick wide pompadour with the ends curled in and waved back.

And No. 3 - A buzz cut with a side-part etched in.

The barber ran his fingers through my hair and tugged at it a bit.

"Hmm…" He growled to himself a few times before speaking out. "Your best bet is number 1. Give it a month and you could rock a number 2. You ready?"

Before I could respond, the barber was already working at my head with a comb and a pair of scissors. He took a few inches off the sides before spraying a dollop of mousse and combing my hair into uniform finger waved perfection. The next time I looked into the mirror, I hardly recognized myself. I looked as if I had stepped out of a 1950s classic movie. Before I could even thank him, I was taken to the next compartment.

"You're welcome." The barber tossed behind his back with a smile as he sat the next boy down.

I was then moved to a man who sat me down and patted my face with a make-up of my shade. "There's always one in the bunch. You gonna do this to me every week, huh?" he shook his head while applying a concealer to my cut and slightly bruised cheekbone.

After a bit of blush and some finishing spray, he bopped my nose with his makeup brush and turned me towards the mirror. I leaned in, astonished.

"I've never seen my skin so clear." I said.

"It's called makeup, darling. No longer just for girls." he said before ushering me out with a wave goodbye.

The next compartment was the largest. There were rows of peach colored suits and tan leather shoes. Still in my underwear, I walked past the clothes and turned at a corner that led to more suits and shoes. After walking a ways forward I made another turn and saw more suits and shoes. Disoriented, I thought there was no way I was still in the warehouse I'd entered a few moments ago. Slowly walking on, I made my way towards a faint nearby rustling.

"Hey, you there!"

Startled, I spun and stood petrified as a man briskly made his way from across the hall. As he neared, I recognized him as the guy who took my body measurements in the beginning.

"I've been looking for you. I have your measurements for your wardrobe." The man panted, breathing heavily. He flipped some papers on a clipboard he was cradling. "Kelley, Brownsfield, Texas, correct?"

"Correct."

The man adjusted his glasses and squinted down at his clipboard. Just then I felt someone walking up behind me. I casually turned to see a man in a peach dress shirt, socks, and absolutely nothing else holding a pair of pants. Wide eyed and quickly turning red, I looked back to the wardrobe master, who simply sighed and shook his head.

"Vous étiez censé à l'ourlet de mon pantalon aujourd'hui!" The man now inches behind me barked, shaking the pants over my shoulder.

"English, please," the man with the clipboard sang calmly.

"I was told you would have my pants hemmed for me if I paid the extra money. When is this going to happen? Je vais être en retard à cause des pantalons ajustés malade!"

"We already hemmed them for you. I told you this last week, they're hemmed to PPR standards. We go in anymore and you'll split 'em on a full bladder. Now cover your narrow ass and get out of my wardrobe before I put you in a zoot suit," the man said with every ounce of seriousness. I tried to fade into the background and away from the situation as covertly as possible.

The nearly naked man then flung himself around and stormed off. "Quelle graisse pâteuse bâtard Amérique vous êtes." He spat, ass cheeks swishing freely in the conditioned air as he sashayed away.

"Goddamn French." The man shook his head and returned back to his clipboard. "My apologies, Kelley. Your suit is Row 5, Number 26. Enjoy your first day!" He looked up and smiled at me warmly.

About twenty minutes later, I was dressed in a smart fitting saturated peach colored linen suit, complete with vest and rich mint colored bowtie. Feeling great, I studied myself in the full body mirror at the exit. This was the snazziest I'd looked since my Aunt Janet's third wedding. There was even something about the fit of the vest that perfected my posture and forced me to poke my chest out a bit more than I usually would at my most confident. My hair looked extra red in this shade of peach, which I didn't care for, but whatever. I made a mental note not to accidentally run my fingers through my waves and ruin my new hairdo. I also remembered I was wearing makeup and so I simply vowed not to touch my entire head for the rest of the day.

I was about to exit the warehouse when something on the floor caught my eye. It was about the size and width of my thumb and it was the deepest orange I'd ever seen. At first I thought someone had dropped a brooch or a piece of fur off their garment. It looked like a cheesy puff someone had dropped from their bag of chips, only it was moving.

I crouched over and watched it squirm across the floor. Suddenly, I recognized it from the wildlife class during orientation. It was a tropic acraga coa. Up close it looked soft and almost gummy. I bent over and nudged it into my palm before exiting the warehouse, and carefully walked off the paved pathway to the nearest tree. I opened my hand and as if the caterpillar instinctively knew where it was better off, it crawled out of my hand and onto a low branch.

"What the hell, may I ask, are you doing?"

I turned to see a tall wide chested man in a peach outfit and mint tie. His tan skin looked as tightly wound as his jet black hair was pulled and wrapped into a clean man-bun on top of his head. His look of almost perplexed disgust nearly shamed me so much that I immediately began to apologize without really knowing what I was apologizing for.

"I'm sorry. I'm- I don't even… I'm so sorry."

"You're not sorry. You apologize. Can you even comprehend how late you are?" He asked very slowly and very clearly as if I didn't understand English. "Was that bug truly worth you nearly losing your job on your first day?"

I could feel my ears turning red. "It wasn't the bug…I mean, it wasn't just the bug…" I stammered.

"Oh? What else could it have been? What's a few more wasted minutes! Entertain me." The man said with a slight scowl.

"I was held up by a naked Frenchman." I blurted. I didn't mean to be so frank but it was all I could say.

The man closed his eyes and nodded, knowingly. He raised his hand.

"Say no more, please. Just follow me," the man said, and without another word or response he turned on his heel and walked briskly off towards the monolith with me following silently behind him.

"How are you doing this morning?" he asked after a moment, keeping his pace.

"I'm doing good. How are you?"

"You are not doing good, Kelley." The man corrected. "Doctors are doing good. The sun above us does good. You are doing well, young friend. I want you to elevate the way you speak, and the way you see yourself. You have been given this position not by chance, but because we see something special in you. With some polish, you will be a high societal expert of five-star guest service. It's awfully hot out here, isn't it? Let's start, shall we."

We entered the building and walked down a dimly lit stairwell that led to a number of tunnels. Each tunnel was labeled and color coordinated. We turned down a blue lit tunnel that was labeled 'SOUTH LOBBY' and silently walked for what seemed like 30 minutes. Every now and then we passed small groups of people either talking in hushed tones against the tunnel walls or walking past them in the opposite direction. Eventually we approached a door and pushed through into an extravagantly decorated corridor. The walls in the French style foyer were lined with an ivory satin wallpaper printed with rose gold vines and flowers and what appeared to be lemons. There were fresh bouquets of exotic and vibrant florals everywhere. The ceilings were high and spacious with cathedral style arches. Even though the space was relatively empty, I couldn't help but creep cautiously as we walked across the gold and white marble floor, but when I caught a glimpse of myself in a portrait mirror near a decoratively placed end table I realized I blended in perfectly. We walked up two flights of stairs and entered a large glass greenhouse garden attached to a massive balcony overlooking the jungle and ocean. The sign in front of the garden read in big swooping letters: *Tigerlily Tea Haus*

"This is where you'll be spending the remainder of your internship," the man said, slowly coming to a stop and turning to me. "I am Massoud, the food and beverage manager here at Le Grand De La Reese. This is the Tigerlily Tea Haus, the most prestigious tea room in the western hemisphere. Here, our guests have the privilege of dining amongst over 50 different species of rare and exotic flowers and their choice of two gorgeous backdrops."

Massoud gestured to the open lobby where I noticed the intricate gold detailing in the arches, which upon closer inspection looked like they were made out of large shards of stark white porcelain. On the opposite side was the walk out patio where outstretched jungle and endless ocean were in plain sight.

Just then a burst of loud hearty laughter came from a side door in the garden and four plump middle aged women strolled in with two large baskets of linen napkins and silverware. Ignoring us completely, they plopped the baskets down on a nearby sofa and continued to gab on.

Massoud called out. "Ladies, Good morning. We have a new intern here at Le Grand. This is Kelley. He has been assigned to Tigerlily Tea to assist you in your daily responsibilities."

I stepped forward and managed a polite "Good morning."

Most of them gave no acknowledgment of my presence, except for this tiny tawny skinned lady, who looked in my direction and cooed a wispy "Hello baby," in a thick French accent before immersing back into their discussion. I wasn't completely sure why, but something about the provocative gestures they were making with their hands and hips made me hesitant to initiate small talk.

I felt Massoud tug on my sleeve just then before leaning into my ear.

"These old hens are the best at what they do and their job will not, I repeat, will not make yours easy," Massoud hissed. "If you can't handle it, or they don't think you can, you will be fired. Understood? There is no other place here at this resort for you. Their ways are now your ways. Their rules are now your own. Follow instruction. Be polite. Learn fast. Understood?"

I nodded wordlessly until Massoud's silence prompted me to speak. "Yes Sir."

Massoud locked eyes with me, his brow thick and overlapping. His eyes searched mine frantically for a split second before returning to his tight faced poise. "You'll be great. We just gotta steer you clear of the caterpillars." The left corner of Massoud's mouth curled ever so slightly.

A smile? Was that a joke? Nah.

"Have a glorious day, ladies!" Massoud called over my shoulder before walking out of the garden and disappearing down the hall.

I stood there awkwardly for a moment before being waved over by this woman with a thick blonde ponytail and an awful lot of mascara for 11 o'clock in the morning.

"You're going to learn to fold napkins. First things first." She said as I took the chair across from her. Her name tag said Kimberly from Ashland, Wisconsin. I grabbed a linen napkin and tried to mimic the folds and pleats I watched the women perform, effortlessly at lightning speeds.

"That's the first shark attack of the season. Poor girl." The woman with the large chestnut French bun at the end of the table continued her story while polishing butter knives. "Awfully early, don't you think?"

"That's no good. Try again," Kimberly said politely. I unfolded the napkin and restarted my folding.

"So, what do you know about tea, baby boy?" The woman with the thick French accent asked as she snuggled beside me. Her name tag said Nanette.

"Umm…" I thought for a moment, trying to think of tea while simultaneously reverse pleating a cloth I'd already folded twice. "…I know there's white tea…green tea…"

Nanette waved her hand. "Baby, there are over eight different types of teas."

"That fold is too big." Kimberly cheerfully sang, patting my napkin. I started again.

"There's rooibos tea, my favorite, which is often red in color and sweet. There's mate tea, yerba mate…"

"…Every year. I don't go out that far if I even get into the ocean at all…" She then grabbed me by the arm, loosening my grip on the napkin I just folded. "Don't go into the ocean."

"Now now, you're going to scare the boy. No, darling, your fold is inside out. Try again."

"…There's oolong tea, which is also wu long tea, wu meaning black in Chinese…"

"Make that tuck tighter."

"…it's a ceremonial tea. Very sweet and aromatic. Now green tea.."

"…And don't go into the jungle either. I really hate this time of season. I really do."

"Black tea is more so the kind of tea you Americans prefer, especially in the south. Ice cold." Nanette let out a loud cackle into my ear.

"…But everything will be fine again…"

"Come to think of it, do you even drink tea, dear?"

"Oh dear, that's not good at all. It's really not quite that hard. Try again."

"…After the sacrifice."

Beads of sweat started forming on top of my forehead; I was in the heat of feeling flustered when suddenly a girl entered the garden. A hush fell amongst the women as the girl silently made her way past the tables towards the balcony. She wore a white lace ruffled gown and a long flowy silk robe that was tied around her waist. Her hair was knotted into a bun above her head with a white scarf woven intricately into it. As she floated past, the gold and diamonds around her neck reflected rays of sunlight around the room and onto the flowers. I recognized her from last night. Princess Hilola.

I slowly folded my linen napkin while stealing casual glances in her direction. I watched her sit at the farthest table where a hundred strange and viney flowers had outgrown their vases and had completely taken over the wall.

A woman had entered from the back room with a small porcelain teapot and matching cup on a saucer. She walked over to where Princess Hilola was seated, curtsied ever so slightly, and placed the teapot and cup on the table before curtsying again and walking away. She then walked straight up to me. First thing I noticed was her eyes.

They weren't exactly terrifying in a dark soulless void kind of way but I would describe them as starry and almost inhuman. Before I could smile to acknowledge her, she was hovering over me, eyes glaring.

"Hello…" she said in a smooth and breathy voice. "My name is Yasheera. What's yours?"

"Hi, my name is Kelley." I stuck out my hand. Yasheera neither acknowledged this gesture nor did she change her blank facial expression.

"Kelley, it's a pleasure to know you're working here at Tigerlily Tea Haus. I'm sure you will be a great addition and adhere to our many rules. The first rule you will learn is that in the mornings when Princess Hilola comes in for her tea and breakfast, you are not to speak to her, you are not to serve her, disrupt her, speak of her, or even look at her for too long. I'm sure you're a great boy with tons of important things that you feel you have to say, but please know that you slip up on these rules once, even on accident, I will not only see to it that you are removed from Le Grande De La Reese, but you might find your replacement job, I don't know, cleaning vomit out of a urinal…that's only if you're not sent home immediately. Do you understand me, Kelley?"

"Y-Yes. I don't want to cause any trouble," I stammered, shaken.

"Excellent." She continued, with a smile. "If you need any help at all, feel free to come to me. Looking forward to working with you." She waved goodbye and set off back through the kitchen doors.

"Don't worry, baby. Not everyone here is as wound tightly as Massoud or Yasheera." Nanette patted my knee.

"Oh, that one is good!" Kimberly gleamed. First I looked over at her, unsure what she was referring to, then I looked down at my napkin to find it folded perfectly.

I placed it in the basket along with the others and grabbed a fresh linen. After about my 8th one, I began to sneak glimpses over at the Princess. I watched her sip her tea and gaze off into the distance. Then, as if she could feel me looking, she glanced over at me. I cast my eyes down for a moment, then when I thought enough time had passed, I peered over again, only to lock eyes. I managed a shy half-smile. She mirrored the expression back at me, only something about it felt weird. I wasn't sure if I'd imagined it or not but I could've sworn that as Princess Hilola began to smile, a few closed flowers behind her slowly opened and outstretched their petals. My glance shifted from the Princess to the flowers, which were not moving, but were now fully bloomed, which I knew they were not moments ago. The Princess returned her gaze to the outside horizon.

After hours of wiping tables and washing teapots, I settled in for lunch in a break room underneath the resort via one of the many tunnels. There, I met a girl that worked in the gift shop. Her name was Dawson, from Winnipeg, Canada.

"This sucks." She said flatly, in between bites of her toasted meatloaf sandwich.

"The job…or your lunch?" I asked, both exhausted and amused.

"I didn't come here to sell overpriced candles to rich old ladies. I'm a nurse. I could be saving lives."

"Then why did you come? That sounds way more important than candles."

She stared thoughtfully into her bag of chips before she spoke up. "Because I've always wanted to visit Paradise Parks. When I was younger, my mother saved up to take me, but then I broke my arm and that money had to go to hospital fees. I saw this as my chance to finally go. Maybe save up and fly my mother out in a couple months."

"Sounds like a decent reason to be here." I nodded, putting my plate in the dish bin and waving goodbye before continuing my shift.

"Wait!"

Rebecca moved her head around the holographic chess board so she could get a better look at her great grandfather.

"Are you making this up?"

Kelley slowly reached out in front of him and motioned a pawn's move with his finger.

"I told you before I started; whether you believe it or not is entirely up to you."

Rebecca scrunched up her mouth, studying the board. She motioned to move one of her knights, then hesitated.

"Oh," she added, "I need to know if Princess Hilola turns into grandma at the end of this story. She sounds really hot and I need to know if mental boundaries are required."

Kelley coughed a chuckle. "No she wasn't your great grandmother, and yes, she was very hot. Maybe the hottest girl I'd ever met at that point. Youth has a way of wrapping turbulent, raw, and wild emotions into shiny harmless packaging. Everything that mattered so much back then matters very little now. Doesn't mean it was insignificant. If anything it means you've grown from it."

They sat there in silence for a beat or two.

"Go ahead," Rebecca said quietly.

"But I've already moved, " Kelley said to her, puzzled.

"No!" Rebecca groaned. "The story, not the game. I already know I'm going to lose."

Kelley smiled. "You've gotten better."

"You can thank Monclair for that when we get back." Rebecca sighed.

"Still not speaking?" Kelley asked with concern.

"Not exactly. My messages are now being received, so she's finally turned on her transmission, which is a good sign, I guess. She's just yet to respond." Rebecca said, staring far past the board.

"Keep trying," Kelley advised, nodding.

Rebecca nodded, too. She then focused on the chessboard, which was now slowly spinning in mid air. Rebecca flicked it out of sleep mode and after a moment, she moved a pawn across the board.

"Good move," Kelley complimented her.

Rebecca looked surprised. "Yea?"

"Well, good enough." Kelley moved his pawn and captured her rook.

Rebecca slouched in her chair.

PART 7 - EVE'S APPLE

I could hear the party from the other side of the door, but I didn't care.
I was covered in sweat, pollen, tea, and was incredibly exhausted.
Leaning against the door, I struggled to insert the key. After a few
attempts, I finally opened the door and sauntered past the group of
Brazilians dancing and grinding to a reggaeton beat that shook the
walls. I passed the twins who were sharing a double header beer bong.
They were covered in paint and wearing large feathered headpieces. I
wasn't sure what they were celebrating, but one thing I learned since
moving in was that César and Fausto rarely needed an excuse to throw
a party.

"Kelley!" César called out and drunkenly followed me to my bedroom.
He slumped against the door frame and took a swig from the plastic cup
he was holding while I got undressed. "Come, have a drink with us."

I untucked my shirt and unbuttoned my pants. I caught César eyeing
me up and down, but I was far too tired to feel bashful or
uncomfortable. I took off my pants and adjusted my boxers before
removing my shirt and putting on a pair of red flannel pajama pants.
"I'm pretty tired, César."

"Do you work tomorrow?" He asked, circling the rim of his cup with
his finger. His gaze everywhere else but my face.

Suddenly I realized, "No…" I said, before putting his shirt on. I'd been
working six days straight and had completely forgotten I had off-days
coming up.

"All the more reason to celebrate with us!" César cheered with a wide
smile.

Edvin walked in and slumped against the opposite end of the door
frame beside César. He was carrying his own cup and his face was beet
red and sweaty. "What kinda peep show is going on here?" He

drunkenly feigned disapproval, wagging his head back and forth. "You paying to watch him strip? How much? I could use the extra money."

César grabbed Edvin's cup and drank the rest of its contents, then he finished his own. "Bring the bottle." He nudged Edvin away. "…and bring Kelley a cup."

Edvin soon came back empty handed.

"Fausto has the bottle. He wants us to come out to the balcony," he said before stumbling away. We followed him past the crowd out onto the apartment balcony. There, we found Fausto and two girls sitting on the concrete floor. One of the girls was stabbing an apple with a pen while the other was applying hair moisturizer to Fausto's dreads from a jar nestled in her lap.

"Kelley, my friend! You're just in time. How was work?" Fausto smiled up at me as we sat down and formed a small circle in the darkness. I pulled my attention from the girl sucking chunks out of the apple and hollowing out the tunnels she created.

"It's been two weeks and it's not gotten easier at all. I overseat tables when I'm hosting, I dropped a teapot of passion fruit tea that stained the floor, and don't even get me started on working in that closet they call a kitchen." I ran my fingers through my scalp out of frustration and fatigue, messing up the pre approved hairdo made that morning. I knew I sounded pitiful and looked disheveled. Though I didn't mean to, I couldn't escape the fact that things weren't looking good for me there.

"You'll be fine. You're smart…and American. You'll be fine." Fausto chuckled. He pulled a bag out of his cargo shorts and fiddled with it.

Edvin patted me hard on the back. "This time next month, you'll be a bored and unstimulated robot, mindlessly executing the job at the required level, just like me."

"Não o meu melhor , mas vai começar o trabalho feito." The girl with the apple said to Fausto as she handed it to him and wiped her hands on her jean shorts.

"É lindo." Fausto said as he examined the apple. Then he grabbed the bag and opened it. "Do you smoke, Kelley?"

It took me a moment, but I eventually realized what was happening. "Um, no. Not really."

"Just tonight then," sang the girl now braiding Fausto's locs. Everyone chuckled. "It will help with your sorrows, poor American boy."

"How blessed you are." Fausto loaded the apple pipe, put it to his lips and lit the top. The glow of the burning weed grew as he inhaled. He then passed it back to the girl, who threw her hair back and took a hit. She then handed it to me.

"Mmmkay…" the girl said, exhaling a ribbon of silver smoke before handing me the lighter. "You hold the apple in one hand. Cover the carb with one finger. No, not that finger. Use the closest finger. It's right there. Why are you doing it weird?"

Edvin was struggling to hold back his laughter.

"Ok, that looks right." The girl said.

My lips pressed against the cold skin of the apple, I watched the leafy embers glow as I inhaled. Everyone silently watched as I held my breath until I couldn't any longer and a plume of smoke escaped from my face followed by a coughing fit I couldn't suppress. The girl beside me smiled and offered me my own cup to drink from.

"For your throat." she said.

My chest was on fire. I accepted the cup and took small sips while I passed the apple to Edvin.

"So you see Princess Hilola everyday. What's she like?"

I wasn't sure who in the circle asked, so I directed my response to the group. "She's quiet. That's how I know her. Every morning she comes up to the tea haus and sits in the same place and has tea. She stares out at the ocean with this look on her face…It's either boredom, contentment, or sadness. Or a mixture. I can't really tell. Anyways, she sits there for about an hour until her entourage comes in and trashes the place and ushers her out."

"OHMYGAWD!!" One of the girls let out a yelp, startling everyone. I then felt tiny talons latch onto my thighs as she lunged from across the circle and into my face. "Was Khamarri there???" She shrieked.

"Who?" I was thoroughly confused.

"Khamarri." César let the nearly glowing white smoke swirl and swim from his mouth and through the air. "He's the tall, dark and handsome one that gave you that olho roxo."

I felt my cheek bone, where the skin had now scabbed and a small thin slit remained. "Oh. Him. Yeah, he was there."

The girl that was previously latched onto my thighs flung herself back and melted dramatically across Fausto's lap, completely possessed by her thirst.

"Ugh." She groaned. "I've never wanted someone so bad. If I ever felt him inside me, I'd die!"

Fausto handed her the apple and lighter and ran his fingers through her long hair. "I can do everything you want him to and more, Gata." He said, real soft and smooth through the darkness, as if it were just the two of them. She cackled and coughed in his face.

"Oh por favor. My life is already unfortunate enough."

We all laughed. I nearly fell over in a fit of giggling as if it was the funniest joke I'd heard in my life. Fausto snatched the apple and lighter from her hand and took a deep hit.

The next day, my roommates and I set out on our rare day off together to explore Paradise Parks and every privilege it had to offer. The sun was high and sweltering as we filed in along with the hundreds of other guests eager to pass the crown of massive canary yellow scapolite crystals protruding from the concrete at the entrance. Paulie galloped and shuffled around excitedly like a toddler, taking pictures and collecting souvenirs. He bounded over to us with a high quality camera he'd just purchased from the gift shop swaying around his neck once we were all in and snapped a selfie of us all together. We made goofy faces and took turns taking photos using his fancy new camera. The energy was light and irrefutably optimistic.

The park was packed. We pushed past screaming kids and tourist groups before reaching the main square just between the volcano and the beach. I recognized the spot from the season opening ceremony footage we watched during orientation. I craned my neck upwards and shielded my eyes from the afternoon sun to get a good look at the volcano. It was crazy to think just weeks ago they were inside of it, meeting Princess Hilola. I was also very well aware that not everyone looking up and taking pictures will ever see the inside of it. I secretly felt like a spy pretending to be a tourist. Pretending not to know the ins and outs of how the park works. We had already run into a girl who was in my orientation class. She was working at an ice cream and cotton candy stand. She welcomed us into the park the way she would to any other guest, then she covertly slipped me a handful of free ice cream coupons with a wink before moving onto the approaching family behind us. I moved out of the way to allow an older lady to capture a better picture of the volcano and retreated back to my roommates in the main square.

I stood next to Keith and peeked over at the amusement park map Fausto was holding. Paulie and César soon joined the group as well, their hands full of large golden brown waffle cones piled high with assorted colors and flavors of gelato. Keith, brow furrowed in concentration, nibbled at the chocolate chip cookie dough with eyes fixed on the map.

"Ok…" he finally looked up and surveyed the crowded scene. He removed his bucket hat and patted his brow. "If we go backwards past the kiddie rides, we should be in prime positioning for The Wave and Pyrotastic."

"I'm down." Edvin licked his mint chocolate chip from underneath his black umbrella.

We did everything there was to do at the park that day; we rode The Wave twice, we entered a terrifying cave where we saw artifacts of the island's mythology and saw the skeleton of a massive four-legged flamingo panther with broad shoulders and jagged fangs. We went into the museum of HUNAM Corporation where we saw some of Ricardo

Hunama's earlier inventions, and saw black and white photos of him with two little girls, both holding wicker baskets of lemons. We even got our pictures taken with the beloved Papayago. He danced around in front of a line of a hundred people waiting to get a moment with him. After waiting 20 minutes in line, we gathered around Papayago as he tousled our hair and pretended he'd known us our entire lives. His face was jovial and very warm, complete with vibrant colors and adorned with tropical flowers. After the photos were taken, he hugged us each and sent us on their way with literal kicks to the butt.

Stripped down to our trunks and Edvin's umbrella, we stood waist deep in the crowded wave pool at the park's water oasis. Old surfer style music blasted from the speakers as children splashed by and a group of girls around our age waded past us, laughing as the cool blue water wrapped itself around their bare midriffs. One girl caught Fausto staring at her and at first she gave him a look of annoyance, but before he could look away, a small smile manifested and her eyes sparkled. He smiled, too, and waved just as she'd turned her attention back to her friends and eventually was lost in the crowd.

"Cruel summer." He sighed to himself before rinsing his face off with cupped hands of pool water.

"Kelley, tell me again, what's the tea garden like?" Paulie asked. He was holding a brightly colored kiddie fan with whizzing foam blades to his face.

"It sucks but—"

"No no," uninterrupted Edvin. He raised his hand and applied more sunscreen to his nose, which looked funny because he was already underneath an umbrella. "I make it a rule to not discuss work on my off-days. I suggest you guys do the same."

I nodded. "Eddie's right…"

"Edvin," Edvin corrected.

"…who's hungry?" I crouched down a bit and let the incoming wave wash over my shoulders.

"I could eat." Keith wiped some hair out of his face.

"We know." César and Fausto said in unison before bursting into laughter, rubbing Keith's perky round belly.

"Piss off!" Keith yelled playfully as he swiped a splash of water into both of their faces.

Just then a rather large wave emerged from the wave pool and glided swiftly in our direction. As it approached, we could see something caught in the currents, and at mere feet away they realized it was the figure of a person. We backed up, instinctively.

"Oh no." Paulie warned.

"Watch out!" A small voice alerted as a head poked out from the wave. Someone screamed and before anyone could get away, we were bombarded as the wave crashed down on our heads. I felt my body spiral backwards and my knuckles skimmed the bottom of the pool. I kicked off the bottom and reached the surface, coughing the water out of my nasal cavities before registering my surroundings. I saw Edvin pick up his mangled umbrella floating nearby. Then I saw Kalu, the young native from outside Cobalt Quarters, holding a boogie board and trying to shake water from his ears.

"Damn it, Kalu!" César rubbed a red spot on his temple where he may have scratched the bottom of the pool.

"Sorry guys!" Kalu rubbed the back of his head and smiled, bashfully. His buds nearby hooped and hollered, splashing wildly. He turned and encouraged the crowd. After several efforts to fix his umbrella, Edvin finally threw it towards the boys, defeated.

"Yo Kalu, anything we should do on our day off?" Keith asked, handing Edvin his soaked bucket hat.

"Too kind." Edvin muttered, putting it on.

"Ummm…you guys been to the fairgrounds? It's pretty cool. The best place to see the sunset. Old people love the sunset."

The guys looked down at him.

"Thanks, Kalu." I sighed.

"Bye guys!" Kalu screamed before catching the passing swell off in the directions of his friends.

Later, as the sun began to set, we strolled the fairgrounds. We were sun drained, ashy, and covered in salt, but we were elated. I took one last bite of my roasted turkey leg and looked up at the golden blushing sky. Everyone was cheering Paulie as he tried tossing popcorn into César's mouth as I wandered off a bit towards the trash can. I threw the turkey bone into the trash and suddenly something stirred inside of me. I looked up from the floor and there, some distances away, sat the volcano, squarely before me. It's ridges and trails etched out in golden lines from the sunset. The tip silently shrouded in a golden pink haze. I couldn't take my eyes off of it. I didn't say it out loud because I know how it sounds, but it felt as if I was being watched. I felt like the volcano was watching me.

PART 8 - CURSE OF THE 7,000 DOLLAR LIMONCELLO

I tried as hard as I could to hide the yawn seeping from my face as I stood at the edge of the gigantic ballroom. I shifted the empty silver tray under my arm and tugged at my tuxedo vest. When I volunteered to work the Investor's Banquet at Le Grande De La Reese, I wasn't aware that it would go on late into the night and 4 hours past my initial shift. At least the tips were good and the next few off days were closer by the second. I caught myself zoning out and did my best to focus back into the room. I watched couples dance in their tuxedos and ball gowns to elegant tropical jazz played by the live band. At this point, everyone was quite drunk and inhibitions were low. I watched these presumably wealthy men chase skirts and roughhouse as if they'd just received their fraternity rings.

Regina Hunama was there. She glided across the marble ballroom floor in a tight black gown and several red flowers in her hair. I wasn't quite sure if they were orchids or not. They looked to be orchids, only I'd never seen orchid petals so blood red. She greeted and waved at everyone with this gigantic, perfect and completely artificial smile plastered on her face the entire night. The only time she removed it was to whisper curtly into Massoud's ear. Massoud, who was mostly attached at Regina's hip most of the night would then scurry off and relay Regina's complaint to whoever the complaint was aimed at, whether it was a server who held a tray too low or too high, or to the chefs about the quality or quantity of hor'dourves.

And of course Princess Hilola was there. Dressed in a 60s style golden dress and white gloves, she remained the center of attention for everyone there under the age of 35. By now I was rather comfortable being in her presence. I casually glanced in her direction and saw her giggling behind her hand as someone enthusiastically told the group a story. Suddenly Papayago waddled by and began to mimic their movements behind them. Everyone burst into laughter and took out their cell phones to snap photos. Princess Hilola gave Papayago a big hug and posed for photo-ops with him before he jigged off to entertain the crowd on the dancefloor. Even I had to chuckle at the way Papayago was dancing and carrying on.

As the night grew old, and the party started to come to an end, I traded my silver tray for a plastic trash bag and was picking up cocktail napkins off the floor when Massoud shuffled over to me.

"I hope you enjoyed yourself. You did well." He nodded in approval.

"Thank you. Yes, I had fun." I smiled, silently reminding himself to never volunteer to work a banquet shift ever again.

"Excellent." Massoud said as a knee-jerk reaction, seemingly uninterested. "Listen, I know you're exhausted. We all are. But I'm going to need you for one more thing before you can go home."

My eyes were fixed on Massoud. My smile was quickly sliding off my face, and I really didn't have the strength to plaster it back on. Massoud, now well acquainted with the ways I showed attitude, concentrated on an imaginary rogue string on the sleeve of his tuxedo and continued talking.

"Princess Hilola is going to be making an appearance at another event tonight on the other side of the island, and I need you to deliver a couple of bottles of limoncello to the club promoter. Afterwards I'll have her driver drop you off at your home. Your apartment is along the way and it should take no more than 45 minutes of your time. You can rest until her driver arrives."

Massoud motioned over to a nearby waiter, turned cleaner and gave him my trash bag. The cleaner, a short boy with blonde hair and dark blue eyes, must've overheard the entire conversation because he took the trash bag without a word and continued on with his duties.

"If you're hungry, see if there's any food left in the kitchen." Massoud told me before walking off across the hall.

"Thanks," I said, flatly. I looked over at the boy, who eyed me silently with a look of sympathy across his face.

"I'm so done." I whispered to him before dragging myself to the kitchens.

I walked into the back and stood in the corner and out of the way while a dozen sous chefs were cleaning and breaking down their stations. My eyes darted from figure to figure until I saw who I was looking for.

I managed to make my way over to a young woman sous chef with warm brown skin and a loud laugh. Her name tag said Heather, from New Orleans. She was the one who delivered the pastries to the tea haus and quickly became my favorite person to have lunch with. Most of the chefs acted like they were curing diseases, but Heather genuinely enjoyed cooking food and feeding people. She was the only one that didn't make me feel like an incompetent and uneducated airhead in the kitchen, and I appreciated her tremendously for it. Plus she fed me, and that's really all it took.

"Hey Heather, how was your night?" I asked, playfully sliding into her as she wiped down a metal counter.

"Not too bad." She grinned, still focusing on her duties. She rarely ever stopped doing her job to talk, and I didn't mind, mostly because it always looked hectically busy in the kitchen. "Took longer than I expected, but I'm glad the kitchen's closed. How was serving? Are you swimming in tip money?"

I scoffed. "Yea, right! I barely got any *thank you*s let alone tips. The only tip I received tonight is if I invented a pill that grew hair and gave an erection, I'd be a billionaire. I'd call it Multi Grow."

Heather exploded in a loud silky laugh that put a smile on my face. Mission Accomplished.

"Hey, is there any leftover food?" I continued.

Heather looked up from her counter and eyed me. "I tried to save you some, but they took it all to the composter."

"But there was so much!" I groaned.

"I think it's all in the back going through spoilage right now. You may still be able to get something if you hurry," she answered, shaking her head. "Oh! I almost forgot…Grand Slam came in to do spoilage."

I was on my way to spoilage when I stopped in my tracks.

"Shit."

The spoilage room was basically a room where uneaten food was counted, then disposed of in a machine that shredded and compressed the food for what I assumed was to be used as compost for the lemon fields.

I entered the room and found myself face to face with Grand Slam, pen and clipboard in hand, counting the uneaten food on a table beside him. Grand Slam was the master chef of Le Grande De La Reese. He was a short, round, ugly little man with a patchy beard and red acne scars across his cheeks. He treated everyone with a holier than thou arrogance and I interacted with him as little as I possibly could. Even Massoud himself rarely went into the kitchen for fear of having to put up with him.

On the table were two trays; one of assorted pastries and tarts, and the other was stacked with roast beef and white cheddar slider sandwiches I'd been serving all night.

"Good evening, Mr. Grand Slam." I said casually as if we were friends. My eyes darted from Grand Slam's massive second chin to the remaining trays of sandwiches and pastries. "How was your night?"

"How can I help you, intern?" Grand Slam said flatly. Before I could speak, he raised a hand to me and finished writing on the clipboard. He then grabbed a sandwich and threw it into the compactor, which churned for a moment before resting at a low buzz. "You were saying?"

I could feel my mouth getting dry and licked my lips. "I just wanted to know if there was any leftover food."

"Tons of leftover food." Grand Slam tossed another sandwich into the compactor. "Oh, are you hungry?" He asked, feigning concern. He tossed another sandwich into the compactor.

"Yeah." I shrugged, pretending to seem unfazed as I watched the blades of the compactor completely shred the sandwich. "Only if you can spare anything."

"Hmm, I think I can spare something." Grand Slam gazed over the thinning pile of sandwiches. He dug through them, tossing each one he touched into the compactor. It churned and shook. After a moment he picked up the entire tray and dumped the sandwiches into the open mouth of the compactor. By now I was trembling with anger. The audacity. The amount of food wasted was already staggering, but to add insult to injury, they'd rather throw it away than feed their hungry employees. I took a couple deep breaths in an effort to control my emotions. After the sandwiches were long gone, Grand Slam inspected the tray as if there were another sandwich hidden somewhere. "Hmm." He mused, sarcastically.

"Forget that I asked." I spat as I turned to walk away. I didn't realize that a bunch of sous chefs had been watching behind me. Their faces and forearms covered in knife scars, sneering and smirking as they blocked the exit door, trapping me in.

"Whoa whoa now," Grand Slam said, innocently. "I'm sure there's something here I can give you. It's been a rough day for you. Holding a tray 'n' all. My chefs don't get the leftovers, but I think you Front House people think that's all we do back here. Cook and eat all day. Now if you were working for me, I'd kick you out of my kitchen and off the island, but you're just ignorant. Hold out your hand, intern."

I reluctantly held out my hand as Grand Slam picked up the tray of dessert pastries and placed a tiny pineapple shaped chocolate pastry in my palm. He then tossed the rest of the pastries into the compactor. I stood there frozen, looking down at the pastry then up at Grand Slam.

"What do you say?" he chimed.

"Thank you." I said lifelessly, before stuffing it in my mouth and swallowing after a couple of bites.

"You're very welcome, intern, now get the hell out of my kitchen and stay out unless you have official business here." I turned around and strolled past the snickering sous chefs and exited the kitchen without saying a word to Heather, who was too busy sharpening her knives to notice me walk by.

After storming out of the front doors of Le Grande De La Reese, I quickly unfastened my bowtie and inhaled deep breaths of the cool wet night air. I was surging with anger and was trying my best to calm my emotions. I doubled over, placing my hands on my knees and allowed the tension in my neck and shoulders to loosen. There was no reason to be humiliated like that, especially in front of fellow coworkers. At that moment I hated the chef. Genuinely hated him.

"Hey cowboy."

I looked up and saw Princess Hilola standing across the walkway. She was chewing bubblegum and clutching a shawl over her shoulders. I straightened up and tried to regain my composure.

"You okay?" She asked.

"Yes, I'm fine. Thank you." I turned to walk back inside.

"Wait," the Princess called out. "Don't you work in the tea haus?"

"Yes. It's a beautiful place." I responded, dryly but not trying to sound too angry either.

"My favorite place on this entire island. It's the only place I don't have to pretend to enjoy." She looked off into the distance for a moment before blowing a gum bubble then sticking it on the nearest trash receptacle, a large amethyst crystal cluster growing out of the ground. "Thank you for leaving me that peace, by the way. I really appreciate it. Usually they don't let interns work in the tea haus...especially boys...but I guess they finally got it right."

Suddenly, Massoud walked out carrying four bottles of yellow luminescent liquid. This, I assumed, must've been the limoncello.

"Here you are." Massoud handed me the bag just as a shiny black town car pulled up to the resort entrance. The driver, a large man in a black suit and tie, got out and strode over to the back passenger seat, where he opened the door and closed it after Princess Hilola entered. I was about to enter the car when my arm was abruptly grabbed by Massoud.

"Listen, this is very expensive resort merchandise. Make sure the right person gets it, understand?" He said in a low voice, casual enough to cause no alarm, but threatening enough for me to respond in an equally low and serious tone.

"Yes, sir."

"Marvelous!" Massoud smiled and patted me on the shoulder and opened the car door. Slightly stunned, I could only muster a small smile as I entered the car and drove off into the dark of night.

We rode in silence. I was completely spent, like most nights leaving my job. It wasn't getting easier. Every day I was facing a new problem I'd never encountered before and had no clue how to handle. And it was always stupid stuff; just the other day some lady deemed it the appropriate time to alert us of her nut allergy only *after* eating two helpings of our chicken salad tea sandwiches, which was often more walnuts than chicken. She managed to call me a useless American twat and demand I be fired right before her throat closed and turned the richest shade of purple I'd ever seen on a human face. Hours later, after she'd received her hypodermic shot and was carted away by the ambulance, I wasn't fired but was still scolded for not asking about any possible allergies as if that was something that we normally did. And to top it all off the lady was offered a complimentary stay at Le Grande De La Reese "for all the trouble we put her through". So the resort can offer thousand dollar rooms to anyone who so much as stubs their toe but my life and employment is threatened all because I haven't eaten and may want a stinky little sandwich that was just going into the garbage anyway?

This place could get all the way bent.

The driver spoke, suddenly, fishing me out of my nightly rage spiral. His European accent was thick and he spoke a lot louder than necessary.

"Well this is exciting. We are in for a crazy night?" he asked.

"You know me. Life's one big party," Princess Hilola answered nonchalantly, not even looking up from her pearly white polished nail bed.

We'd been driving out through the jungle for miles when there was a sudden dull pop and the car shook violently before coming to a complete stop.

"It's the bloody carburetor," The driver spat as his head popped up from the hood of the car. I wiped the sweat beginning to trickle down my forehead and repositioned the flashlight I held just above his shoulder.

"I said that earlier," I muttered, shining the flashlight directly in the driver's face. The driver fixed his mouth to say something foul just when Princess Hilola stepped out of the car.

"Princess, please stay in the car. For your safety," the driver cautioned, loosening his tie.

"It's hot in there," she retorted casually, leaning against the car. She pulled her phone from her clutch and as the screen light illuminated her face, I was again stunned by her beauty; her face was dewey from the jungle humidity and even in a moment of inconvenience, she looked cool. She had no bad angles, no distinguishable imperfections, and even being one of three people stranded on a road in the jungle, she commanded attention so effortlessly.

"No signal." She shoved her phone back into her clutch.

I pulled my phone from my pants pocket and checked the screen. "Same."

Look at us. So compatible.

The driver started nodding. First to himself as he looked down at the smoking car, then to the two of us.

He raised his hand and gestured to me. "Okay. Just stay calm."

"I'm calm." I nodded back, aware that the driver might be beginning to lose it.

He then swung his hand over to Princess Hilola and gestured at her. "Don't panic."

"I haven't panicked in weeks." She shrugged and pushed the stray hair from her face.

"You two stay here, and I'm going to walk back and get help."

"You're going to leave us here?" Princess Hilola asked, suddenly alert. "Do you really think that's a good idea?"

"You and I both know what's in the jungle, Princess," he said to her, uncharacteristically blunt.

"Why do people keep saying that?" I said aloud, annoyed.

"You have the safety of the car. I shouldn't be too long."

Princess Hilola fell silent, and after a moment, she nodded. "Be safe."

He walked off back towards the resort. Princess Hilola and I watched him until he was enveloped in the darkness.

Princess Hilola pulled a small bag of nuts from her clutch purse; she struggled to open it.

"Need some help?"

"I got it, thanks."

The bag popped open and she ate a few almonds before offering me the rest.

"I imagine this doesn't happen often." I asked, popping a few salted almonds into my mouth.

"This has only ever happened to me one other time." She said, "Two years ago I was stranded off the eastern shore on a yacht. It just wouldn't start back up! I was about to consider swimming to shore when I spotted a coast guard boat coming towards me. The coast guard on duty also happened to my ex boyfriend at the time. This 6'6 guy, with gorgeous brown hair. He was a big beautiful, incredibly dumb boy. I like them a little dumb." She smiled.

Amused with her storytelling, I couldn't help but smile as well.

"Anyway, he was drunk. Too drunk. He boarded the yacht and was very unhappy with me. He said we weren't going to get to shore until we were back together."

Princess Hilola took a dramatic pause and stared out into the dark jungle.

"We don't have to talk about this," I said solemnly.

Princess Hilola snapped from her trance and popped a few almonds in her mouth. "Oh, it's fine. That's not how this story ends. He ended up drowning that night, and I used his boat to get to shore. Totally auspicious coincidence, ya know?"

I looked down at my shoes and nodded, grappling internally with my urge to ask what happened. I decided it was best I let it go.

"This year 15,347 people between the ages of 18 and 30 from 124 countries all over the world traveled to this island for work, for opportunity, and for experience." Princess Hilola said casually, as if it had been drilled into her memory. "I'm curious, what are you here for?"

I looked up to speak and noticed Princess Hilola standing frozen in place, her eyes fixed on something. I followed her gaze, and what I saw made my mouth drop: a large yellow orb of light, 4 yards away from where we stood, moved behind the branches and vines of the jungle. It quickly shifted and changed shape as it glided past leaves and over tree roots without making a sound.

"What is it?" I whispered, my eyes wide and fixed on the orb, which thrashed about, expanding and contracting.

Princess Hilola moved her head in my direction, her eyes still locked on the orb.

"We aren't in danger…but stay very still."

The yellow orb got brighter and larger, and it was moving closer. I began to feel my heart beating faster. I could feel my legs beginning to shake.

"Maybe we should get in the car." My voice cracked nervously.

"Shhh" Princess Hilola held her hand out towards me. "Just trust me. You don't have the answers. Stay where you are."

I wiped the sweat from my forehead and stood my ground. The orb grew closer. And brighter. A slight buzzing and rustling of leaves. Brighter still.

Something clicked in my head and I bolted for the car. I threw myself in and closed the door behind me.

"Princess, please get in!" I yelled through the glass. She didn't even acknowledge me.

She remained stationary, watching the orb grow. It shifted violently in size and shape. Only a few feet from the car, I could then see that the orb was a thousand smaller lights swirling and…

Fireflies.

They moved like a cloud over the car as Princess Hilola walked over to the passenger side. She opened the door and leaned down to look me in the face. I could barely contain my shock and embarrassment, but I met her gaze and braced for the ridicule and laughter.

Princess Hilola stared at me long and hard and in total silence before she spoke.

"If we run from the things we don't understand," she whispered, "and fear the things we run from, aren't we just running our whole lives?" She held out her hand.

I nodded, sheepishly, and took her hand as I exited the car. Together we watched the firefly swarm for a moment as it swirled over the road and made its way back into the edges of the jungle, forming a yellow orb surrounded by darkness.

Drowning in silence, I finally spoke.

"I partially blame you for me panicking, you know!"

"Me?!" She balked, a grin quickly appearing across her face. "I told you to stand perfectly still and you deliberately disobeyed!"

"Yea, only after all that talk between you and the driver about the 'dangers' of the jungle." I protested warmly. "What's out there anyway?"

Princess Hilola shrugged. "It's a jungle. It reveals less and more of itself everyday."

"Deep." I said, playfully. She shot me a knowing look.

Two stray fireflies whizzed past my face towards the front of the car and down the beaten road.

"Grab your things, you big scaredy cat."

Princess Hilola took off her heels and adjusted her dress. "We're walking."

Without any hesitation, I picked up the bag of limoncello bottles and we set off down the road.

Eventually our eyes adjusted to the deep dark blue shade of the moonlit night as we got comfortable enough to converse. Princess Hilola talked about growing up on the island and her favorite food.

"In the summer my father would make an emerald crab ceviche and I can eat that ceviche every day for the rest of my life."

"Would? As in won't make it any more?" I asked.

"Not since Paradise Parks really started getting big. He got involved in the corporate aspect of it all and didn't really have time for crab hunting." Her voice lowered towards the end.

I felt a moment of sadness but… "Wait, Paradise Parks was founded in…1963-"

"1965." Princess Hilola corrected.

"1965. That would make you…how old?"

Princess Hilola laughed cooly. "Has no one ever told you it's rude to ask a girl her age, much less a Princess? Massoud would have your head."

"My apologies," I adjusted my shirt collar. "It's just that there's actually people here that believe that you're the same actress from when their parents were children. That's crazy, right?"

"What's crazy is that you brought that limoncello with you. We have at least 3 miles ahead and I know it's heavy."

I'd completely forgotten I had the bag containing four large glass bottles of the yellow drink. They were heavy. I adjusted my grip on the straps and continued on, completely unaware of Princess Hilola's deflection.

Princess Hilola and I talked about what our schooling experiences were like (public school vs. royal home school) and we talked about our moms.

"I never knew my mother. I have pictures of her. She's a beautiful woman." Princess Hilola told me. "What's your mom like?"

I looked off into the darkness. "My mom died five years ago. She was a victim of gun violence. Some idiot purse snatcher…life sucks like that."

"I'm so sorry, Kelley." Princess Hilola whispered.

"So am I."

Suddenly there came a low growl some distance from us followed by a rustling of the bushes that made us both stop in our tracks. It was muffled and seemed to be buried somewhere off beside them.

"Please tell me it's another swarm of fireflies."

Princess Hilola shook her head. "Definitely not fireflies. Walk slowly. Don't make eye contact with anything. In fact, don't even look into the jungle right now."

We picked up pace and walked in silence until it felt safe. Eventually the chirping of birds and monkeys returned to the surrounding jungle, which was a good sign that nothing nearby wanted to eat it.

Moments later, we arrived at the gates of Cobalt Quarters. When we got to the apartment door, I suddenly remembered my roommates and spun around to face Princess Hilola. My arms extended out, blocking her from the door.

"Princess, do you mind waiting here? Just for a moment? It's an apartment of six guys. It's not exactly Le Grande Del La Reese in there."

After a tense stare down, she let out a sigh and nodded.

"Hurry up." She mumbled.

I used my key to unlock the door and discreetly slid into the apartment.

I entered and shut the door behind me. When I turned around I saw exactly what I suspected: Edvin cooking in a mess of a kitchen wearing nothing but his boxers and a large ridiculous chef's hat. Keith, also in his boxers, was clipping his toenails on the couch. Fausto was sitting beside Keith, completely engrossed in a soccer game on TV.

Fausto was also in his boxers.

"Why is everyone in this apartment half naked!!??!" I yelled as I scrambled to grab trash and clothes off the floor.

"Technically, we are half dressed." Edvin said thoughtfully as he stirred the milky white paste that I could only assume at the moment was soup.

"Well I need all of you to go get dressed! Put some bottoms on at least!" I pleaded with them, stuffing trash down into an already full trash bin.

"Relax." Keith scoffed, shifting attention between me and the soccer match. "What're you on about, mate?"

I looked them in the eye, seriously. "I've got a girl outside."

The three boys all smiled and nodded.

"Ah, you don't want her to come in and see all this beefy competition." Edvin lowered his voice and did his best to flex his muscles. "I understand!"

"No, I don't think you quite understand." I shook my head and slowly raised a finger pointing to the door. "Princess Hilola is on the other side of that door."

Fausto chuckled, his eyes still glued to the TV. "She's that hot, huh?"

"No," I spoke slowly. "The ACTUAL Princess Hilola is currently standing outside our apartment complex waiting to come in."

Fausto, Keith, and Edvin were now giving me their full attention.

"Bollocks!" Keith spat loudly and very suddenly.

"I bollocks you not, dude! She's out there waiting so I need you all to either get dressed and help me clean or at least put on shirts!" I pleaded, delirious. Blame the lack of sleep and food, but I knew I had the face of a madman trying to keep it together and what was worse, I didn't care.

"Wait, wait, wait." Edvin put down his giant wooden spoon and placed his hands on his jutting hips. "Why would the Princess of Paradise Parks want to come home with YOU?"

Now wide eyed and panting, I zoned in on Edvin.

"Oh? As opposed to YOU? You goddamn chopstick!"

"Whoa baby, whoa!" Keith held out his hands if I just triggered an earthquake. He tried to remain straight faced, but Edvin did look chopstick-ish.

Edvin slammed the spoon on the counter. "Chopstick! Listen, you fat American-"

"No, you listen!" I interrupted. "No one is scared of you, Edvin. What is it with you cooks?

"Cooks?!!?" Edvin yelled.

"Cooks! You're all so rude and have no social skills!" I spewed the thoughts from my head.

"Guys, chill out!" Keith tried to pacify the situation, but his intentions were lost in his loud cackling and his attempts to get his phone in the perfect position for recording.

"What's bollocks mean?" Fausto asked aloud, contorting his face into confusion.

We were so consumed in the heat of the moment, no one noticed when Princess Hilola walked in.

"I couldn't wait anymore, I have to use your bathroom. Also it smells amazing in here." Her soft velvet feminine voice completely dissolved the testosterone in the room and we were frozen in silence as she walked past and into the bedroom.

Edvin tried to casually cover his nipples with his arm as he pretended to concentrate on his soup.

When Princess Hilola returned from the bathroom, everyone was dressed and in a more cheerful disposition. We sat down at the table over what Edvin called a potato soup topped with cheese and fried shallots.

"Not bad for a 'cook'." Edvin hissed as he ladled two big spoonfuls into my bowl.

I nervously stirred. "Are you sure you want to stay here tonight, Princess?"

Princess Hilola was wearing an old shirt and a pair of shorts from my closet. Her hair was in a low ponytail.

"Totally sure. If I go back to the palace tonight they're going to want a full report of what happened, and then a bunch of people who got the night off will be called in and it'll be this whole unnecessary thing. I doubt they even realize I'm missing. Trust me, this is the better option. Only if you don't mind, of course."

"I don't mind!" We all said in perfect unison. Princess Hilola smiled.

"You know what this meal needs?" Princess Hilola got up and grabbed the bag containing the bottles of limoncello. Almost immediately, Fausto got up and grabbed a few cups from the kitchen.

"No." I found myself saying. "That stuff's expensive and if Massoud finds out that the club never got it…"

"Massoud has a lot more to worry about than a few bottles of alcohol. Don't worry about him." Princess Hilola popped open a bottle and poured everyone a glass. We all picked up our cups and held them for a toast.

"To the island." Princess Hilola sweetly, just loud enough to be audible. We tilted our drinks back against our lips and let the silky limoncello wash over our tongues. It was a dark heavy lemon flavor that was almost balanced with a light airy hint of vanilla bean. I exhaled deeply as the alcohol fumes were trying to escape through my nostrils.

Just then the front door jiggled and opened as Paulie came limping in. My eyes widened when I saw the bandages wrapped around the top of his head and the blood spots that had seeped through them above his right eyebrow.

"¡Puta merda!" Fausto yelled.

"What the bloody hell, Paulie?" Keith got up and rushed over to his roommate to help him sit at the table. "What happened, mate?"

Paulie, though distressed and disheveled, smiled and seemed to be in good spirits. His eyes were clear and bright, though dark circles surrounded them.

"I'm alright. Don't worry too much." He shrugged and began to dive into the bowl of soup Edvin placed in front of him. "Today was actually a good day."

"Where do you work?" Princess Hilola asked.

"Nature control." Paulie looked up from his bowl and his eyes grew wide as he realized he was sitting across from Princess Hilola. He waved at her, then modestly grabbed a slice of the French bread from the center of the table and took a huge bite before focusing back on his meal.

"I see," Princess Hilola said, nodding more to herself than to the other boys, who all looked sick with concern for little Paulie.

"Your friend is absolutely fine." She waved them off and took a sip of her drink.

"He doesn't look too fine." Keith watched Paulie as he slurped at the soup and inhaled the bread as if he hadn't eaten in weeks. I noticed that he did seem thinner than the last time I saw him.

"I assure you, he's fine. All nature control rangers are going through the same thing. The first month or so are the most rigorous days, and he's still alive so he must be doing well," she said in an easing tone, gesturing to his lively body as proof.

The three of us were fixed on Princess Hilola, stunned by her words and casual demeanor.

Paulie pushed the now empty bowl away and grabbed the open bottle of limoncello. After sniffing at it for a few seconds, he put it to his lips and took a few large swigs before coming up for air.

He wiped his mouth on his already dirty sleeve. "Welp!" he chimed, with a wild smile. "Goodnight guys!" And just like that, he limped off to the room with the bottle clutched close to his chest. He then turned towards us and bowed at Princess Hilola before slamming the door behind him.

"We've got more." I assured Keith, who seemed offended and shocked by Paulie's behavior.

Five empty bottles later, we were strewn across the living room.

"So why do you do it?" I asked, flatly. "If all the parties are pointless and everyone is stretching you too thin, why don't you just put a stop to all of it. If this isn't all pretend and you truly are the Princess of this island, then you have the power to do whatever you want, right?" I folded my arms.

"It's not that easy. It really isn't," Princess Hilola said quietly, body flailed over the arms of our lazy recliner chair. "It's my job, and it's a job only I can do. It's funny, as a child I was told I was going to do whatever I wanted as an adult, and the older I became, the more I realized that being an adult is getting up and doing all the things you don't want to do. Even when you have the option of not doing them." She leaned up a bit to look into my eyes. "It's choosing that unfavorable choice that shows how much you've grown."

"Unfavorable…" I said aloud, pondering her choice of words. "You're so smart. That's rare for pretty girls." I joked, in an attempt to compliment her, tease her, and flirt. This skill I could usually only do two out of the three.

"You're kind. That's rare for straight white boys." She smiled and lifted herself up off the couch.

Caught completely off guard, I cackled. "Hey! I'm only half."

"Half white, or half straight?" She asked rhetorically as she stretched upwards towards the ceiling. "Thank you, Kelley, for being you."

"Thank you, Princess." I responded drowsily.

Princess Hilola made her way to my bedroom, where she closed the door behind her. I nestled deeper into the sofa. I couldn't believe all that had happened that day, but I was far too tired to process it all. Just as my eyelids grew heavy, a slight glimmer caught my eye. Before I could focus on it, it was gone in the darkness of the room. The still and rhythmic breathing of my roommates nearby pushed me toward a deep sleep. I wasn't even sure if I was still awake when I saw the glimmer again. The second time I saw it, I knew what it was almost immediately. One single firefly.

I awoke to César singing loudly and quite beautifully in Portuguese off in the distance and sun rays from the blinds dancing across my face. I lifted my heavy head off the couch and staggered towards my room. The door was open and the room was empty. The only trace of Princess Hilola was a faint floral smell I'd never smelled there before.

Day - 15 - Bowviolet Space Shuttle - 181 hours until Earth Landing

Rebecca let the warm water run down her body as she stood in the shower and thought of what the Princess told her great grandfather. Lately she felt like all her choices were unfavorable with little growth to show for them. She tried to think of the last time she did something for herself, because *she* wanted to do it. She pushed her hair to the side and massaged her shoulder as the water beat down. She couldn't remember.

After her shower she got dressed and joined her crew in the media lounge for a movie. Some classic two-dimensional film about a brunette girl and a blonde boy from two feuding families. They fall in love despite the odds.

"Did they really talk like that in the 1990s?" Quan leaned over and whispered.

"No…At least, I don't think so."

After the film was over, she checked on her great grandfather who was sound asleep, then retired to her own chamber. There, she ruffled her blue hair and made an attempt to log her day.

"This is Captain Rebecca Dodge. Day 15…"

She checks the time.

"…Hour 2. The ship is stable, en route to planet Earth."

She leaned back in her desk chair and gazed outward into her thoughts.

"Things are good…but that feeling of…dread. I don't know…impending doom? I'm not sure what it is exactly. I promise, everything is fine. I just have this sense of fear. Fear of the future. Fear of the unknown. Fear of what's coming next. End of log."

The recorder pinged, signaling its completion. Rebecca's heart was pounding.

It had been a great few days off: we woke up and decided to trek towards one of the more popular waterfalls in the jungle. The sun was still rising when we packed our lunches, filled our canteens with water (Fausto filled his with wine), and set off down the trails. The jungle canopy was lush and the trail was spacious enough that the birds and monkey's echoed in the trees.

"Not so terrifying in the daytime." Edvin exclaimed with a smile as he wiped his wet hair from his forehead.

"Do you think we'll run into Paulie?" Keith asked. Now that Paulie was living in the appointed nature control barracks, he had the room all to himself but it had become obvious that he missed his roommate sometimes.

"Maybe." I kept pace in the rear of our group. "Do you think Paulie knows that you cry at night all alone because you miss him?"

Fausto and César chuckled.

When we arrived at the waterfall, I was astounded by just how tall the cliff was. The water cascaded down the moss covered rocks and freefell a seven foot wide downpour into a pool not much deeper than four feet. Best of all it wasn't crowded. There was a family of five playing on one side and a group of teenagers hanging out on the other, so we decided to camp in the open space in the middle. We kicked off our shoes, tossed off our shirts, and placed our things down before wading into the murky blue pool towards the waterfall.

We let the cold water beat down on our heads and down on our shoulders, soothing our mosquito bites and cleansing us of the alcohol enriched sweat that had been leaking from our pores the entire hike. I looked over to see Fausto grinning ear to ear, his brown curly hair covering his eyes completely.

Water logged and exhausted, I sat at the bank of the waterfall. I watched the family play in the pool. They were a beautiful family; a couple in what looked to be in their early 40s and their three happy children splashing about-

"Emery?"

One of the girls from the group of teenagers at the other end of the waterfall was calling out to her friend. I casually looked around but didn't see anyone. After a moment, one of the girls came up to our group.

"Hello, I'm sorry to bother you, but there was a guy with us. He's tall with dark brown hair…have you seen him?" She asked.

We all shook our heads. I surveyed our surroundings again while she moved on and asked the family if they'd seen him as well. The pool was shallow and the water was clear. He couldn't have drowned, and if he did we would have found his body, but there was no sign of him. He'd even left behind his shoes, his shirt, and his phone. Were we led to believe he decided to take a stroll through the dense jungle without any shoes or belongings? I suddenly became very uneasy.

"We'll help you look. You said his name is Emery?" Keith got up and asked.

We all looked within a 10 yard radius of the waterfall, and we double-backed on the trail. No sign of him. His friends grew more frantic, shouting his name as they trudged through the jungle. The overall mood at the waterfall had shifted and the visiting family promised they would send Nature Control to the waterfall before promptly leaving. Within an hour, a squad of nature control officers had arrived and were taking professional search and rescue measures around the surrounding areas. We only stayed long enough to see one of the Nature Control officers gather information from who we learned was Emery's girlfriend. She was sobbing uncontrollably and could barely produce the information the officer needed for her paperwork. I overheard one of the officers mention this was the third case of a person vanishing in the jungle that week, but we were escorted back on the trail and left for home before I got any more details.

Days later, after a pretty easygoing eight hour shift, I was called into Massoud's office. It was a clunky cluttered place, full of stacks of various maps and brochures and open mail envelopes all over the place. After a moment, Massoud entered the room and sat at his desk. He didn't respond when I greeted him, and after making a faint effort in organizing the scattered items on his desk in silence, he finally looked up at me.

"So, tell me what happened that night after the party," He demanded.

Almost immediately my heart sank and my mouth began to dry. "We were on our way to the party when the car broke down. The driver said he would go get help and Princess Hilola and I waited for quite some time before we decided we were better off walking towards my apartment."

"Princess Hilola spent the night at YOUR place?" he asked in disbelief.

I nodded.

"Why didn't you call the hotel when you got home?"

"Um…It's- it wasn't something…we didn't think to do that at the time." I was visibly searching for the words.

"…Or anytime at all during your days off?"

I could only shrug. "We didn't think of that at the time."

Massoud added with a defeated sigh. "Well, what happened to the driver?"

"I don't know." I told him, now perplexed. "Wait, he didn't make it back here that night?"

"No one has seen him since the three of you drove off 72 hours ago." Massoud sighed. My eyes widened as I searched Massoud's face.

"What?" I asked, more urgently than I actually intended. "What does that mean?"

"What happened to those bottles of limoncello I sent with you?" Massoud asked, completely ignoring my question and concern.

I regained my composure. Truth is, I knew this moment was coming and I thought about what I'd say but I still didn't believe I'd have to lie to save myself. "I left them in the car. When we left I had completely forgotten about them."

"Oh? Well when they found the car, it was empty. So…" Massoud nodded, drilling his glare straight onto me. I pretended to dust something off my pants in an effort to break the staring contest.

"I don't know what happened…" I shrugged, genuinely at a loss for words.

Resigned, Massoud continued to nod.

"Kelley, I understand that you had very little control of the events that did and did not happen that night…" he started, quietly and calmly. "…however, I left those bottles under your supervision. That's over seven thousand dollars' worth of Paradise Parks and Resort merchandise just disappearing into thin air. Did the driver who disappeared double back once you guys left and pick them up? Were the bottles swiped from the car before the authorities arrived by some unknown hooligans passing by?" Massoud fiddled with his cufflinks. "Or did you just take them home and drink it all with your roommates?" He casually glanced up at my face. I sat in my chair, frozen. Afraid to even breathe a telling breath. I tried to stop my own heart.

"I guess we'll never know." Massoud continued. He turned in his chair and stared out the window that overlooked the lush green jungle. "I like you, Kelley. You work hard and are quickly becoming a highlight of the tea haus. But actions have consequences." He turned around and slid a paper across his desk in front of me. I peered down at it, still motionless, and read 'Notice of Dismissal' in bold black letters sprayed across the header.

"I'm going to have to terminate your career here at Paradise Parks. " Massoud handed me a pen.

I wordlessly took the pen and signed. I felt empty. It was better to sign the paper now before I could feel the full weight of its meaning.

"Effective immediately, you are relieved of your position here at Le Grande De La Reese and your employment at Paradise Parks and Resort." Massoud sighed, reciting what Kelley figured he must've said a dozen times a year. "You will go to your apartment, pack your things, and at 10:30am a shipping boat will arrive on the same dock the interns were dropped off. You will board the shipping boat and it will take you to the airport. I wish you the best of luck in your future endeavors."

I stood up on my feet and headed for the door. "I'm sorry." I said dejectedly, more to myself. I could feel the color withering from my being.

"What you mean is you apologize. Understand that it was your carelessness that led you down this road, not the situation at hand. You not calling the hotel and reporting back to us makes you sorry. You losing several thousand dollars worth of Paradise Parks property makes you sorry. Being sorry, which is an insult, is the same as being lame, incapable, defective, less than. In this situation, you are these things. But I accept your apology."

I felt all the blood rush to my face as I turned and stormed off without another word. I walked through the nearest exit and let the hot midday sun drench me. I furiously unbuckled my bowtie and threw off my suit vest. How fucking dare him. I worked my ass off and learned so much useless information and now I was being sent home over one night. What did I do to deserve this?

I waited at the shuttle bus stop to take me back to my apartment. I ignored the other interns laughing and talking loudly amongst themselves on the bus ride. I felt so far away from them, like I didn't belong.

When I arrived home I walked past Keith and Edvin sitting in the living room playing a video game. I didn't hear if they said hello or not, but it really didn't matter. I entered my room and stared at my things. Just when I couldn't bear it anymore I grabbed my duffle bag and started removing my clothes from the dresser and shoving them into the bag. My face was hot and I couldn't help but feel sorry — yes, Massoud, *sorry* — for myself. This was all my fault, and now I was being sent home with my tail between my legs all because I didn't think about the consequences. What was I going to tell my grandmother when she had to pick me up from the airport six month ahead of schedule?

I didn't see Keith and Edvin standing silently in the bedroom doorway until moments later. It didn't stop me from packing, but I was beginning to feel like a zoo attraction. The idiot in a cage.

"What's going on, mate?" Keith finally spoke.

I sighed. "I got fired. I'm going home in the morning." I snapped my baseball cap around the leather strap of my duffle bag.

"Are you serious?" Edvin ran his hand through his hair. "What happened?"

I shrugged. "Too much of a good time, I guess." I shook my head.

"Damn. Well…we're gonna miss you." Keith nodded. "Sucks it's ending this way. Do you need help or anything?"

"No…I'm pretty much almost done. Thank you though." I sat on the floor, looking up at them, feeling hopeless. "It was great meeting you guys. Really."

Edvin grew pink in the face, lip beginning to quiver. "This sucks." He said with a pout, and he walked away from the doorway, out of sight.

"Take care of yourself, yea?" Keith said, managing a small smile before backing up from the doorway and leaving me in silence.

After I was packed, I rested on my bed in the darkness. I tried my best not to think of how I knew this would happen, or how to tell my family I screwed up an opportunity like some reckless kid they didn't raise well. Most of all I thought of the nothingness that lay ahead. I had no plans, no dreams, and no direction. Hot tears escaped my eyelids and cooled my cheeks before soaking into the pillow. When my alarm woke me hours later from an empty sleep, I sat up and let my eyes adjust. A part of me hoped yesterday was just a very vivid bad dream, but there in the corner of my eye, I saw my packed bags waiting at the foot of the bed.

I collected my things and quietly left the apartment. I then made my way to the bus that was heading towards the dock. When I arrived at the dock, three other interns were there waiting as well. One girl was facing the ocean, sobbing. There were two people there I did recognize: my intern advisor, Mark, clutching his clipboard and shivering against the morning wind whipping past his bare legs in those notoriously short shorts, and a very tall guy with dark brown unruly hair. As unruly as it was, it still couldn't hide the deep purple and nearly black right eye.

"Way to blow it." Mark sneered as I walked past him with no acknowledgment whatsoever.

"What'd you do, man?" The boy yelled the moment he recognized me, his mischievous grin curling over his cheeks. I parked his stuff next to the boy. I couldn't help but see the poetic irony in leaving with the same person I arrived with.

"Drinks with the Princess." I shrugged. The boy's laugh was evidence enough that he didn't believe me, but it didn't matter.

"Ok, if you don't wanna tell me it's fine." The boy held up his hands. "In that case I'm going home for the drinks with the Princess as well." He laughed. "Nah, my bunkmate ate my ramen and I socked his ass."

"This sucks, man." I looked off in the direction of the rising sun. The clouds encrusted with golden light in the fuchsia sky.

"It is what it is." The boy shrugged. "We weren't going to be here forever." He pulled a blunt and lighter out of his cargo shorts and lit it in between his lips. "At least I wasn't, anyways."

I nodded. "So I guess you're off to medical school now, huh?"

"Law school," The boy corrected. "And no. I'm still not going. I do what I want."

"Someone once told me growing up was about doing the things you don't want to do."

"Yeah?" The boy ran his fingers through his hair and I caught a glimpse of his full face. "Well that person probably doesn't have much control of their life and maybe even looks a little sad at times, huh?"

I thought about Princess Hilola sitting with her tea.

Moments later, the small red boat that dropped us off months ago had slowly pulled up to dock and the captain rang his bell. Everyone on shore began to board in an orderly fashion. I filed in line, preparing to board.

"Kelley Immerson Dodge?" A booming voice came from behind me.

I turned to find an older gentleman in a black suit standing in front of a town car at the edge of the beach. He had an electric megaphone that covered more than half his face.

"Mr. Kelley Dodge, if you're present, I suggest you not board that boat!"

"He was fired and no longer works here, he has to go home!" Mark, the intern advisor yelled back with a screech. He then began to forcibly corral me towards the boat. I was at the edge of the ramp when I felt a hard tug at my arm. I turned and saw the shaggy haired boy pulling me back.

"Don't be stupid. Stick up for yourself, man!" he urged me.

"He doesn't work here anymore. Neither do you!" Mark spat.

"Good observation, thighs!," the boy spat back. Offended and embarrassed, Mark turned to gather the others to the boat. The boy turned back at me.

"What are they going to do? Double fire you? At least go see what the old man wants." He said in a moment of heartfelt seriousness. I looked into his face and I felt my chest begin to swell. I couldn't deny that he was right. This seize the moment attitude was the main reason why I was here in the first place.

I took a step back, away from the boat as it began to slowly float from the dock.

"Thank you."

"Say hi to the Princess for me." The boy smiled before pushing past Mark to board the boat. Mark, who stood on the boat's edge, silently glared at me in disbelief.

I was walking towards the man with the megaphone when he spun around. "Dude, I don't even know your name, but thank you!" I shouted at the boat, which was now yards away. "I'm Kelley!"

I watched the boy move to the back of the boat. "Kelley!" He waved. "I'm Neil, but my friends call me Nova Toad!"

I squinted in confusion as he waved back. "Nova Toad?"

"Nova Toad?!?!" Rebecca nearly choked on her tea. "Now I know you're making this up, you old lying bat."

"I'm not making this up." Kelley stated calmly.

"So you're telling me that the music God, the cult legend…the intergalactic prince Nova Toad of Nova Toad and the Sonar Lilies himself advised you, wait, URGED you to stay on the island? You met the greatest rockstar there ever was?"

Kelley nodded.

"I mean, I don't think he was that great, but I've met him. Yes. He was just a shaggy haired boy I knew of."

"Fine." Rebecca rolled her eyes and took a sip of her tea.

Part 10 - HOLLOW

I drifted to sleep in the back of the town car. When I woke up, I found myself on a part of the island I'd never seen before. I got out and found myself in the middle of what almost looked like a desert. We came to a stop at what looked like a mile of sandy beach. I turned back towards the road and saw the green mountains of the island off in the distance. I turned back towards the ocean and there I saw a small motorboat on the shore and a white yacht floating gracefully farther out. I grabbed my bag and walked towards the ocean. Moments later, I reached the motorboat where I'd met the same old man who drove the towncar. He was leathery and almost bronze-looking, but he had the brightest, warmest smile I had seen since I'd been there.

"About time you woke up," he teased. "Now if you please, we're in a bit of a time crunch." He motioned me towards the motorboat. Within moments were aside the now massive yacht. I admired the polished creme color and macassar ebony detailing. I climbed the rope ladder aboard and was greeted by a full staff. They were all just as bronze and leathery as the man, and they even shared the same smile. I wondered if they were all related. One woman with long brown hair showed me to my living quarters.

"Make yourself at home. We will arrive in a few hours." The woman's velvet voice had the same accent as the local boys that lived near my apartment. I figured she must also be a local.

"Thank you," I spoke quietly. "Where are we going?"

The woman smiled. "You're in good hands. If you need anything, I won't be far." She then left and closed the door behind her, leaving me to my own devices in this yacht suite.

The bedroom was larger than the living room I shared at Cobalt Quarters. There on the bedside was a pitcher of a yellow drink with pink petals swimming amongst the ice. I recognized it as the same drink served on the plane ride to the island. It was sitting beside a platter of sliced meat, cuts of cheese, olives, and of course, lemon wedges. Suddenly realizing how famished I was, I helped myself to the platter and even a few cups of lemonade. Afterwards I showered and got dressed in the clothes that were left out for me on the grand dresser ; a pair of white jeans, crisp new all white high top sneakers (how did they know my size?), and a plain white T-shirt. Dressed and ready for whatever was next, I looked out of the cabin window at the small island we were steadily approaching. I watched as the setting sun made the high island glimmer in shades of pink and green. I let the grand luxuriousness of it all engulf me as I layed down and closed my eyes.

When I awoke, it was by the gentle nudge of the brown haired stewardess informing me that we had docked. I freshened up in the bathroom and was led up to the deck and a drawbridge leading to the island. I thanked the woman and made my way through the twilight of the evening across the bridge onto the island. I then came upon a small metallic cable car that carried me up the mountain. Through the brush and banana leaves, I caught my first glimpse of a crystal palace towering above the highest mountain. I couldn't make out much in the twilight, but I did notice the base being ingested by massive vines, like dark green veins against the pale peach building. My curiosity far outweighed my cautiousness as I pressed against the glass for a better look.

The cable car let me out right in the front yard of the palace. I walked through the garden, past fragrant punch colored amaranth flowers and the largest comet orchids I'd ever seen. My Dad would be in flower heaven! I walked up the stone stairwell to a colossal pair of doors speckled with the same foggy gemstone I'd seen at Le Grande. I knocked on the door and waited. No answer. I thought I heard a muffled laugh from somewhere inside and then more silence. I knocked again. No answer. After a moment, I attempted to open the door and it slid apart without making a single noise. I entered the mansion and pushed the door closed behind me.

I cautiously crossed the long spacious foyer. It was dimly lit by oil lanterns and grandiose candles. All was relatively quiet except for the echo of voices down the hall. The closer I got, the clearer the echoes became.

"Ew, no it burns my nose." I heard a girl's voice say.

"So I'm on top, and she's going wild…" A deep male voice rang out before going into this high pitched moan of sexual "ooh"s and "oh yeah"s before a collective laugh.

"Oh my God, you look ridiculous. Stop padding your crotch."

"That's all me baby."

Then the entire room burst into laughter again.

It was when I entered the main hall did I realize the people speaking were Princess Hilola's entourage. The same feral group I'd seen first at the Volcano party months ago, then nearly everyday at the tea haus. They noticed—but made no effort to acknowledge—me.

The curly blonde haired boy who had previously just been simulating sex furiously on the sofa, flailed back onto the cushions and feigned boredom when he registered my presence. "Oh, it's you." He groaned, coldly, choosing to focus on the details in the cushions embroidery.

They were all lounging about the space, wearing white and gold. Khamarri, the one all the girls obsessed over, glanced at me from the cocktail bar built into the library book shelf. He didn't say anything, just sighed before downing his drink and turning away to make another.

Suddenly I was accosted by the girl with carmine colored hair. She wrapped her arms around my torso and pressed against me in a hug.

"You finally made it!," she squealed as she pushed her thick curls back out of her face. Her smile was wide and made my face hot.

"I'm Kelley." I held out my hand. The girl looked at it, then looked up at me, perplexed.

"Honey, I know." She wrapped my open hand around her waist and pressed in to kiss my cheek. "I'm Tegra. We're so happy to see you. We've been waiting for you." She intertwined our fingers and led me through the main room.

"That beautiful disgrace on the sofa is Ronan," she sang, referring to the blonde boy on the couch. Without looking at us, Ronan raised his hand.

"So THRILLED to have you here!," he yelled, his tone saturated in sarcasm.

I was then introduced to Moncyra, "Cy-Baby'' according to Tegra squealing as if she hadn't seen her in weeks and had no clue she was alive, let alone were in the same room. Moncyra smoothly motioned to the airpod in her ear as she was hunched over in a grand lavender upholstered arm chair painting her toenails a rich blue and setting gemstones into the wet polish.

"Je vous ai dit que je serai là quand je suis là." She purred in between blowing her nails dry.

She tossed her dark chocolate curls to the side and blew us kisses before returning to her nails. "Je ne peux pas attendre de vous sentir ce soir, chérie. Apportez ce que vous avez promis, ok?"

We then strolled over to Khamarri, who was now taking selfies with the blonde girl with starry freckles. Tegra slid in on the other side of Khamarri and I watched the three of them take countless photos. I even tried to join them and was half-heartedly pushed out. After they were done, I was informally introduced to Farrah and Khamarri. Khamarri made me a drink that was without a doubt the hardest brown liquor I'd ever had.

"That's very expensive Japanese whiskey. You'll never get used to it. Do you know why you're here?" he asked, casually. The two girls looked at Khamarri, annoyed.

I did my best not to grimace after a sip of my drink. "No clue. Do you know why I'm here?"

"No clue." he mimicked me, swirling the whiskey in his glass.

"Where is Princess Hilola?" I asked.

"She's close." Farrah teased, sipping from a crystal chalice and motioning at an ajar door in the back of the room. "She's been waiting for you."

"Whatever you did or said has really stuck with her. All she does is mention you." Tegra added, smiling sweetly as she nuzzled herself against Farrah's shoulder.

"It's getting really annoying, to be honest." Khamarri muttered before downing the entirety of his liquor and turning back to the bar.

"Nevermind him, he's just jealous." Farrah threw her hair back. "Go see her."

I thanked them and made my way to the back of the room alone. I walked through the doors and found myself outside on a spacious balcony overlooking the ocean. It was dark, but lit by the moon and a sea of stars, I saw Princess Hilola leaning against the railing. Did she orchestrate all of this, just for me? Why? These questions came flooding into my brain, but before I could speak it was her who broke the silence.

"You see that star? That one there. That's my star," she proclaimed with pride. I could hear her smile before I saw it. I walked behind her as she pointed up into the sky and did my best to trace her fingertip to a singular glimmer amongst the billions, but after a while, I gave up.

"Princess," I began, cautiously. "Why am I here?"

"Are you asking literally, spiritually, or metaphysically?" She teased, glancing back over her shoulder at me.

"Why am I not on a flight back home?"

She turned around fully in my direction, her face reflecting the moonlight.

"There's something about you I like, Kelley. I can't quite put my finger on it. The time we spent together was amazing and I don't get to see that side of people very often on account of my title here. I want you here, with me. I feel better knowing you're here on the island." Her tone was simple and delicate.

Brain spinning and cheeks in full flush, I could do nothing but stand there in the dark. I tried to think of something to say, but nothing I could come up with felt worthy enough to say aloud. A sudden burst of fireworks shook me from my trance.

Princess Hilola shrugged. "Plus, it was my idea to drink the limoncello. I wouldn't be able to sleep at night if I knew my decision got you sent home."

And there it was. I managed a nod. Before I could accept her apology, I was distracted by a low buzzing that I didn't notice at first, but it grew louder and continued to conquer the sounds of the ocean. Tracking the sound, I managed to spot a helicopter gliding towards us in the night sky.

"Tonight is a very special night. I want you to be a part of it." Princess Hilola whispered excitedly.

She strode off into the main room; I followed closely behind. Everyone inside had just finished getting ready as Princess Hilola pressed a button in the corner of the room that lowered a cage elevator. She and I stepped in and everyone filed in behind us.

"Shit, I forgot my clutch!" Farrah gasped and pointed to a small white ostrich feather bag on the sofa. "Kelley, be a babe and grab it for me?"

"Sure!" I nodded, eagerly. I exited the elevator and grabbed the clutch. I turned around just in time to see the elevator gate shut. Everyone was hysterically laughing and waving goodbye. Everyone except Princess Hilola. She just smiled warmly, then pointed to her left as the elevator rose. I looked over and immediately bounded for the stairs. Three flights later, I found myself opening a door to the rooftop where the helicopter had landed and followed Ronan inside. I wiped the sweat off my brow after I secured myself into the seat.

"Hazing, right? So much fun!" I gave everyone a cheesy thumbs up.

Farrah snatched her clutch from my lap and continued to loudly talk with Moncrya who sat beside her. Across from me sat Khamarri, who stared at me cold and unflinchingly as the helicopter lifted off.

As we made our way over the ocean and through the theme park spotlights, my heart wouldn't stop racing. How did I end up in a helicopter with the island celebrities? Their clear skin, toned bodies, and pearly white smiles made it hard to stare directly at them. And they knew it. I would find myself in staring matches where I would constantly lose because I could never bear to share the intimacy longer than a few seconds. Still, if Princess Hilola's way of apologizing was to invite me to live one night as a socialite, then that's exactly what I was going to do. An hour later, we were descending on a landing pad at the edge of a waterfall. As we approached what appeared to be a massive cave carved out of the side of the mountain, Khamarri pulled me aside.

"Listen, the moment you enter our world, you are going to see and hear things you won't believe even though they're happening right in front of you. Some of it is real, some of it is only pretend. Our job is guest experience, and we're great at our jobs. What we provide you're not going to get anywhere else on Earth. You interfere or refuse to play along, that little red tugboat appears on that departure dock the same time everyday and will gladly take you home. Your job is to observe, support, and have fun. That's it. Understood?"

I nodded. "Understood."

Khamarri searched my eyes for a moment, then a wide smile spread across his face. His entire demeanor changed as he wrapped his arm around my shoulder.

"Good."

We entered the cave together and walked down several flights of dimly lit stairs until we reached an elevator at the bottom. The word HOLLOW was carved into the wall and backlit by what seemed like water above the elevator signal button, which Ronan pushed. The doors opened almost immediately, flooding the cave with purple LEDs.

"Kelley, you're in the back." Khamarri said and gestured for me to enter first. Then Princess Hilola followed with both Ronan and Khamarri by her side. Finally Moncrya, Tegra, and Farrah shuffled in up front.

Moncrya pulled a compact mirror out of her bra and checked her makeup. "Shit, I forgot that rock over there. Kelley, can you grab it for me?" She said in a saccharine voice just before the door closed. Everyone snickered at my expense. I even had to smile and shake my head in slight embarrassment.

We felt the elevator come to a stop. I watched from behind as everyone became still, and well postured. Even Tegra, whom I could only describe as hyperactive, had taken on an air about her. It was the very same jaded disinterest I had only seen in teen movies when the popular girls called in slow motion through the school hall, and suddenly here I was drowning in it in real time. There was a chime before the doors opened and a sea of electric blue light washed over us. We exited in unison and walked out onto a small platform runway plank. Everyone in the club immediately turned to notice us as if we'd created a gravitational pull. People were stopping mid conversation to stare. I even saw two people who'd been feverishly making out stop kissing just to throw us their gaze. Astonished, I watched partygoers on either side of the runway fall to their knees, bowing as we walked past.

Princess Hilola stalked forward, the messiah in her domain, completely in control.

I watched as Moncyra, Tegra, and Farrah slinked through the parting crowd like hungry tigers, eyeing everyone with looks of lust and menace. Ronan and Khamarri bulldozed past the sideliners like moving walls of brick. All I had to do was concentrate on keeping a proper distance behind Princess Hilola, even though I felt the thousands of eyes behind me like daggers in my back.

There in complete unison, we walked, effortlessly, through the crowd and past massive stalactite formations rising from the ground that formed around the DJ booth. We reached a platform overlooking the entire nightclub. It was furnished with plush sofas and small tables covered in luminescent moss and ice cold liquors. The room even had a small hot spring that looked extravagantly carved out of the cave wall. Unfazed, Princess Hilola and her friends settled in, making themselves drinks and checking their phones. Eyes wide and mouth agape, I could not hide my awe as I continued to admire the VIP lounge. I'd never been in a VIP lounge this nice. Well, once when my middle school friend Charlie Weaton had a VIP section at his arcade birthday party…but this was way nicer. Way nicer.

I walked over to the balcony and stared down at the crowd of dancing people. These people weren't the awkward looking obnoxious guests I saw waiting in lines at the theme park, nor were they the visibly tired moms and dads who chased their children through the resort. These people were young and vibrant and gorgeous. I caught the eye of a girl on the dance floor. I smiled and she smiled back. Then, without an ounce of hesitation, she opened her top and casually exposed her breasts to me.

"Kelley, can you at least *act* like you fit in here?" Ronan's voice croaked from behind me. Still in shock, I turned around and slowly walked towards the lounging posse, not saying a word.

Several drinks later, Ronan was in the middle of enthusiastically telling one of his many sex stories (complete with visual mimicry) when we were greeted by a tall woman in a business suit.

"Pardon the intrusion, Princess Hilola. Señor Moscado would like to accompany you and your friends this evening."

Everyone at the table—except Princess Hilola and I—groaned a bit. "He's more than welcome." Princess Hilola gave an effortful half-smile, which quickly faded as the woman turned heel and left.

"Who's Señor Moscado?" I asked the table.

"Santiago." Tegra corrected me. "No one calls him Señor Moscado but his assistant."

Ronan downed the last of his drink before motioning for another. "His father is the Honduran-"

"Chilean," Farrah interrupted.

"There is no prime minister of Chile!" Moncyra snapped, looking up from her phone to scowl. "It's a presidential republic, you tart."

Farrah threw a long lock of hair behind her shoulder and shrugged. "Whatever, the title doesn't even matter. Bottom line? The boy is filthy rich, socially awkward, and completely pathetically in love with Hilola. He paid for our presence here tonight."

"So be kind!" Princess Hilola chimed to the group.

Just then Santiago came strutting towards them. He was tall and handsome in a fitted cream colored two piece suit and dark hair coiffed back. His chest poked out dramatically as he walked over, as he came closer the smile on his face was so perverse and intense, it nearly sobered me up. He looked like an overconfident car salesman on his way to screw us over.

"Good evening everyone. I'm so pleased you all could make it to my party." He announced in a thick South American accent. I watched Santiago bow before Princess Hilola and I caught a heavy whiff of floral aftershave.

"Thank you for having us, Santi." The Princess said as politely as she could while trying not to choke on the scent. "I have to admit, I had no idea this was your party tonight. I wish I'd known."

Everyone looked at Moncyra, who pretended to read the label on a bottle of Dom Perignon. I felt Santiago's intense glare on me almost immediately.

"And who, may I ask, is your guest?" He asked through a tight smile.

"This is my dearest friend, Kelley." Princess Hilola leaned over and patted my knee. I did my best at playing it cool; I got up to introduce myself.

"Pleasure to meet you." I extended my hand. Santiago glanced down at it then back up at me.

"Wish I could say the same, sir. I did not plan for any extra guests in the VIP lounge so you would be sitting in my seat, drinking my top shelf tequila from my sipping glass." Santiago smiled through his teeth. We sat there with nothing but the booming music between us.

I had nothing to say besides… "Oops."

This made Ronan and Tegra choke back laughter which turned into full blown hysterics. Even Princess Hilola giggled.

"Now now," she said, trying to regain her composure. "He didn't know. Santi, baby, I'm so sorry. Let's all be friends."

Santiago, embarrassed for his display of jealousy, adjusted his suit coat. "Of course. No hard feelings. Now, shall we dance?"

Drinks in hand, we all made our way down past the DJ booth and onto the dancefloor. Packed into the center, we mingled with extravagantly decorated older women and shirtless young men. Skinny models in box dresses and bearded men in kaftans and man buns. After a moment, Santiago's assistant appeared out of nowhere with a tray of drinks, which Santiago did the honors of passing around to everyone.

"Apologies for my savagery earlier. Just so you know, I fully intend on winning her from you." Santiago leaned in and whispered to me.

I scoffed. "I think you've misunderstood."

"Time will tell. Anyway, let's be friends, yes?" Santiago raised his glass.

Nodding, I took Santiago's shot from his hand then proceeded to down both mine and his. Afterwards I stacked the glasses and politely handed them back to him. "Now we're friends."

Santiago laughed, putting a hand on my shoulder. "Sonofabitch! I'm beginning to like you already!"

We danced in pairs, in groups, and at one point, I watched in awe as everyone performed a solid well-choreographed number. It was unlike any party I'd ever attended. I'd mostly been to college house parties or the occasional EDM rave in the next county over, but this truly felt like a celebration. Papayago even made an appearance, spraying everyone with champagne from the VIP lounge before coming down to join in on the dancing.

I came to at the crack of noon the next day in one of the many bedrooms of Princess Hilola's mansion. My mouth was bone dry and a dull headache was brewing in my brain and turning into the worst hangover I'd ever had. I managed to stagger to the bathroom to wash my face and drink a bit of water from the faucet in an effort to rehydrate. Afterwards I collected my bags and slowly walked down the stairs, careful not to make any noise. I was at the door when I heard steps coming from behind me.

"And where are you running off to?"

Khamarri and Moncyra had entered the foyer from the main room. They were in t-shirts and sweats, Khamarri sported serious bed-head while Moncyra's hair was wrapped in a scarf and she had no makeup on. They both looked strikingly normal.

"Good morning," I began weakly, my voice croaking. "I was just leaving. I had fun last night. I wanted to thank you guys for letting me hang."

"I must admit, you fit in surprisingly well. The Princess knows how to pick 'em." Khamarri spoke softly. "When she hears that you left, she'll be heartbroken."

"What do you mean?"

"We like you, and the Princess wants you to stay. You don't have to leave, like, at all." Moncrya squeaked. "…If you don't want to."

I stood there, trying to wrap my brain around what I just heard. Khamarri read my thoughts and a drowsy smile spread across his face.

"Yeah man, you live here now. Go put your bags back in your room and have a bowl of cereal with us."

PART 11 - LIVING IN THE PALACE.

And so, My new life living with Princess Hilola had been laid out for me by her guardians.

"If you're going to hang with us, the least you could do is look like us." Ronan scoffed.

In the mornings, I would work out with everyone except Princess Hilola. She would already be on her way back to Paradise Parks. This routine consisted of an hour or so in the weight room lifting with Khamarri and Ronan, who completely ignored me initially until I caught up in weight class, followed by a jog around the island with Tegra, Moncyra, and Farrah. This had become the highlight of my morning once I learned to keep pace. I wasn't much of a runner back home, but I soon learned that it cleared my thoughts and I could push the tensions far from my physical self as I ran faster. Also there was a comradery I enjoyed while running with the girls. Most of their jokes were inside jokes I didn't understand, but it was still good to see them laugh and interact outside of the plastic shallow personalities they portrayed in the clubs. Afterwards we'd all freshen up and have a breakfast of fresh fruit and green smoothies before boarding the yacht where we'd get professionally administered facials as we sailed to Paradise Parks.

I was understandably nervous walking back into Le Grande De La Reese for the first few times since being fired. Running into Mr. Massoud was the absolute last thing I wanted. I was assured that everything would be fine, but I couldn't help feeling like a puppy that just walked onto a freshly cleaned carpet.

I entered the Tigerlily Tea Haus behind the gang as they went directly into their ritual of eating and drinking whatever they could get their hands on. This was what they considered their main caloric intake for the day. Warm croissants and cheese danishes were not safe as they strolled by the dining table. My former coworkers, who were busy chasing Ronan and Tegra out of cream and scone saucers, didn't pay me any attention at first. It was Kimberly, eyes wide and plastered with mascara, who noticed me first.

"Kelley, darling…I thought you…" She trailed off, stunned.

"I was." I nodded. "But now I'm…I'm with them."

Kimberly shook her head in anger. "That's absurd. I've just gotten used to dealing with these animals and now they've added another brat to their rag tag team? This is unacceptable. I'm quitting."

I took a step back. I'd never seen Kimberly so angry. I mean, it was somewhat comical, but still startling.

"I'm done! I can't do this anymore. I quit, I'm serious!" She panted hysterically.

"Calm down, Kim" Nanette casually walked by and handed me a raisin scone.

As Kimberly fussed at an unfazed Nanette, I walked over to Princess Hilola and stood quietly behind her as she finished her tea.

"Good morning." She peeked over her shoulder, smiling. Like the sun, I found it hard to look directly at her.

"Good morning," I replied.

Before I could say any more, her entourage had spilled out onto the patio in full force, roughhousing, stealing food, and taking risqué selfies. After a moment, Farrah strolled over and leaned against the top of her armchair. She moved her curly hair away from her face as she swiped on her phone.

"Good morning, Princess! Ok, so there's a wedding in the Siracusa Fields at 2:00pm, your presence is requested for a sunset dinner at Emerald Clif's, and there's a party at Club Iris. That's at midnight. It's optional but the manager has been holding the VIP lounge for you for weeks and is dying for you to make an appearance."

"Relatively light day." Princess Hilola smiled into her cup of tea.

We were all just leaving the tea haus when I, of course, came face to face with Mr. Massoud; he looked up from his clipboard just long enough to lock eyes with me before looking back down.

"Kelley," he greeted, nonchalantly. "Tagging along with the Princess and her gang of feral socialites are we? I have to admit, I thought you were better than that."

"Well I wasn't given much of a choice." I snipped, trying my best to control my anger and mimic Massoud's calm frankness.

"Friends in high places." Massoud nodded. "Careful not to fall."

Massoud walked on.

"Can I ask you something, Sir?" My voice boomed through the hollows of the hall. I didn't want to risk him not hearing me.

Massoud turned around. "Of course."

"When you found out we never made it to the party with the limoncello, why didn't you send out a search party? Surely you were concerned about our safety. What took *you* so long?"

Massoud looked taken aback for a moment, then tried to regain his demeanor.

He searched for the words. "Well, I…Um…I was busy with-"

"The question is now rhetorical, unfortunately." Seething, I bit into the scone and crushed the remainder of it, letting the crumbs fall through my fingers to the floor.

"Have a great day at work." I backed away from him joining Princess Hilola and her friends while catching the look of both offense and disbelief on Massoud's mug.

I returned back to the balcony and in the middle of Khamarri and Ronan arguing about something feverishly but simmered down when I entered. In fact, it seemed as if all the energy had been drained from the group.

"What's going on?"

Princess Hilola put on a smile, though her face looked strained.

"There's been a shark attack on the southern shore."

My heart sank. "Oh no."

"They're ok," she continued. "But sharks on the southern side of the island are…"

"Rare." Moncyra finished her sentence.

"Yes, rare."

"So with the entire southern shore closed down today, we'll just have to move some things around. Princess, I'm rescheduling your dinner at Emerald Clif's on account of…" Farrah tapped frantically at the phone screen.

"…of suddenly not having an appetite." The Princess put her teacup down with a thud, clearly frustrated in thought.

"Right." Farrah agreed, cautiously.

"We'll catch up with you guys later." Khamarri tugged on Ronan's sleeve as they prepared to leave.

"Should I go with you guys?" I asked.

Everyone except Ronan looked at Princess Hilola.

"Yeah! Let him come. He wants to be one of us." Ronan had a big fake grin on his face.

"Ronan." Tegra warned, her voice uncharacteristically low.

"No, you stay with us." Princess Hilola got up from her chair and tilted her head as she stretched her neck. "We'll see you guys later. Go now. Don't be late."

Khamarri and Ronan walked briskly off the balcony and out of the Tea Haus without another word. I looked at the ladies in complete confusion.

"What just happened? There's something you're not telling me."

Moncyra giggled, "There's A LOT we're not telling you."

"Don't worry about it," Farrah linked her arm around my waist. "You're spending the day with the girls."

"Think you can handle that?" Tegra ruffled my hair and with a chuckle we exited the Tea Haus for the spa for sauna and seaweed wraps.

Eventually the other guys joined us and we were back on schedule as if nothing had happened. Even Ronan was in a slightly better mood, so I let it go.

Every day wasn't like this. Usually after retrieving Princess Hilola from tea, we would spend the days in the company of those who could afford to keep us. When we weren't yachting with descendants of royalty, who dared us to help spend their ancestral inheritance on frivolous purchases, we were having business lunches with Fortune 500 companies and fancy dinners with diplomats as if they were all old friends. We attended weddings, sweet 16s, bar mitzvahs, and various day parties for various occasions. I quickly realized that Princess Hilola and her gang of hooligans were the perfect addition to any event they attended. Expertly mixing socialite immaturity with skillful and effortless schmoozing, they were able to cause a stir and be the center of attention without getting out of control. They never got too drunk, never seriously offended anyone, and they were always happy to be there. Having been the tagalong, I was tolerated at most. I didn't mind most times, because it gave me a front row seat to the theatrics. I watched Ronan and Khamarri compete for the affection of a prime minister's daughter at her 60th birthday soiree. I watched Tegra slide off the hood of an eight million dollar Maybach Exelero while they were hired to model cars at a Mercedes Benz auto show. It was hilarious. Every now and then Santiago and his assistant would join us, and would either slow us down, or change our plans entirely if he could afford to outbid the initially planned event. Princess Hilola would never seem bothered, she'd smile and adjust. I learned that Santiago was happiest when he was talking about himself and when he was happy, he was a lot easier to be around, so I let him unload his boasting and his ego driven exaggerations onto me and in turn he wouldn't pester the Princess. The group was grateful for my patience and tolerance and were extra friendly with me whenever he was around. I'd finally found where I was most useful.

On one occasion, we were invited to dinner at Le Grand by a famous Greek film director in an attempt to appease his teenage daughters who were enamoured by the Princess. The dinner went off spectacularly, and when chef Grand Slam himself visited the table to prepare our dessert of bananas foster and saw me sitting there, he nearly scorched his chef's coat.

We rarely had days off to ourselves, but when we did, we spent our time lounging about, eating junk food, and I spent a great deal of time exploring her personal island. One of my favorite days together was the time we'd built a picnic of fruit, wine, and cheese and laid out under the sun on top of one of her island's highest mountains. We trekked for hours through the jungle and the rocky terrain to finally reach a cleared patch of grazing grass on a cliff overlooking a small cove and miles of ocean. Listening to Tegra's sweet singing voice being carried off by the wind and Ronan's accompaniment on Spanish guitar, I have never felt more at peace. Everyday I spent with Hilola was a different, often surreal version of paradise.

One morning I woke up to find the palace completely empty. When I went to the dining room, there was a duffle bag and a note on the table.

Kelly,

The misspelling of my name had to have been on purpose. How childish.

Sorry we didn't wake you. We've got different plans today. Grab a little breakfast and the duffle bag. The helicopter is waiting on the roof! See you later!

The letter wasn't signed, but instead was kissed by blood orange stained lips.

I grabbed the duffle and a pear from the fruit basin on the table and took the elevator to the roof. There awaited the helicopter. Once aboard, I was carried to the northernmost point of Paradise Parks, and was dropped off on a small cliff overlooking a beachside wedding reception with several of the wedding guests wading in the dark blue waters below. I walked to the edge of the cliff where a girl sat, her long curly brown hair flowing in the high winds like I'd seen it flow several times before. It has become one of my favorite images.

"Hilola." I called, with a smile. "What lesson shall I learn today?"

I sat beside her and opened the duffle bag. After a moment I retrieved the pear and gave it to her. Princess Hilola looked down at the pear and smiled before taking a large bite and giving it back.

"Kelley, you're having fun, right?" she asked, wiping juice from her chin.

"I'm having the time of my life," I managed through a mouthful of pear I had bitten off for myself. "I want to thank you again for saving me. I don't know how I'm ever going to make it up to you."

"Don't thank me just yet." She smiled out into the horizon, a faint hint of sadness flitting in her eyes. I noticed it, and watched her silently before she spoke again.

"Hey, I wanted to show you something," she chirped. "You're a strong swimmer, right?"

"Well, I was a lifeguard one summer at the local-"

My voice gave out as Hilola flung her shirt off over her head, revealing a dark blue bikini top, and kicked off the edge of the cliff to swan dive gracefully into the ocean below.

At first, I shrieked from shock. Just as I was convinced Princess Hilola had just killed herself, I sighed, relieved to see her spring up to the surface of the ocean in a fit of giggles.

"You know you've gone insane, right?" Kelley called down to her.

"Come on, Kelley Kelp-For-Brains!" she shouted.

"Kelley Kelp-For-Brains??? Ouch!"

"That's what the kids are calling you on the streets!"

"Well damn!"

I stood up and with my heart beating rapidly, looked over the edge down at the ocean underneath. After making sure no swimmers were in my way and no rocks protruding from the cliff, I took a few steps back.

I took off my shirt and looked up at the sky. Suddenly as if I'd left my body, I watched my legs make a running kick off the edge of the cliff. There I was, airborne, gasping for oxygen before plunging feet first into the blue.

Completely submerged, I opened my eyes to see the ocean bursting and vibrant with activity; schools of tiny fish moved in zigzags, dodging the bare legs of swimmers wading through the water. A sea turtle, who appeared out of nowhere, tugged at the pocket of my denim shorts. I dug into the pocket and pulled out the pear core, which the turtle snapped up and swam away. A few feet beneath the turtle, I noticed a bit of movement on the coral bed. A swarm of dark brown hair catching the sun's rays. I swam down and after a closer look I saw it was Princess Hilola laying in a massive half clam shell. She then blew me a kiss and swam off. I went to follow after her but was halted almost immediately. I looked down to find a thick scarlet tentacle wrapped around my ankle. The tentacle was attached to a large octopus anchored on a nearby boulder. After a few efforts in freeing myself, I kicked at the tentacle with my other foot and once I was free, I shot the octopus the middle finger before swimming off. I looked around for Princess Hilola but saw nothing, so I shot for the surface.

Gasping for air, I wiped my face and looked around. After a moment I saw the Princess sitting at the base of a small cave near the cliff. She was too busy detangling her hair with her fingers to see me swim up. After I was able to find my footing and climb in, I followed her as we ventured into the cave. It was dimly lit and the rock floor was smooth and cold. The narrow tunnel soon opened up wide enough into a standard sized hallway and I began to notice that the lighting was not natural, but coming from behind lanterns disguised as rocks.

"Where are we?" My voice echoed, though I was whispering.

"Shhhhh…" Princess Hilola hissed.

We then encountered a man-made flight of stairs that led us down into the entrance of a pub style tiki bar. The cave walls were decorated with what were either glass windows or television screens that mimicked views of the ocean reef and the room was well lit with home lamps and neon signs.

Princess Hilola wrapped her hair in a bun and took a seat at the bar. "Good afternoon, Palo. Two dark and stormys, please." She smiled at him.

"But of course, Princess." Palo bowed before grabbing two glasses.

I joined her at the bar. Just when I realized how shirtless and cold I was, a cocktail waitress walked by with two towels and two shirts for them that read 'ENKI BAR'.

"It's the name of the bar. My father's favorite bar on the island," Princess Hilola said, throwing on the oversized shirt and placing her towel on the seat. I followed her cues, and did the same.

"Your father…the King." Kelley confirmed.

"No," Princess Hilola smiled. "I married into royalty. My father was far too cool for all of that. King Kalbar may have ruled the island, but my dad was king of Paradise Parks. In the 70s my dad and my uncles and all their friends would gather here and get wasted and gamble and talk shit about their wives. It was a gentlemen's club. Now it's mine." She looked around at the patrons, who mostly consisted of old couples and swimmers coming in from the ocean for a drink or to use the bathroom. "Mostly it's just one of Paradise Parks' hidden treasures now."

She picked up her drink and took a small sip, then dug into her wet denim short pockets. After a moment she pulled out two gold coins and handed them to Palo. He bowed and retreated back to tending the bar.

"He makes the best drinks," she whispered to me. She raised her glass. "You are my guest, so you get the first toast. What shall we toast to?"

I picked up his glass and thought for a moment. "To the island."

"To the island." Hilola nodded and we both took gracious swigs.

Suddenly a slow melodic song echoed through the cave. I looked around for the source of the hauntingly alluring sound, but could not place it. I began to see the pub's patrons excitedly hovering over the glass aquarium windows. Then, just out of the corner of my eye, something big swam past the window, but before I could get a good look it was already gone. It appeared in a window across the room, then was gone again. All I could catch a glimpse of was a large wide tailfin. And fingers. I could've sworn I saw fingers. I looked over at Princess Hilola, who beamed, grinning ear to ear.

I got up off my barstool and walked over to one of the glass windows. I peered through it, searching the clear blue waters, and there after a moment, swam a mermaid. In clear view was a stunningly gorgeous girl with shimmering dark hair wearing a wreath of seaweed and shells over her bare chest. Her tail was a lush green and covered in millions of reflective scales. Though I figured it must've been a swimsuit, the grace and effortlessness in her movements made me second guess myself, if only for a second. She twirled and swam on her back while mouthing the words to the song being played. Her gills stretched across her rib cage, vibrating.

I caught her eye and she swam over to the glass where I was. Heart pounding as she drifted on the opposite end of the window, I managed a smile, which she returned. I noticed her eyes were dark blue with pupil slits like a snake's. She kissed the glass passionately before pushing off and continuing her swim around the bar one more time before disappearing off into the depths.

Dazed, I walked back to my seat. Princess Hilola stared at me unflinchingly as I took a large sip of my drink, barely unable to conceal her happiness.

"So how the hell did you do it?" I finally asked after a moment.

"Do what?" Princess Hilola shrugged, eating a few fries that'd been brought to us in a basket.

"The mermaid show we just saw. The eyes. The gills! The fact that she lasted so long underwater without air. How did you pull it off?"

The Princess cleared her throat.

"When guests come to the island, they're immersed in a mythological world. The volcano, the jungle, the parties…me." She smirked. "Now, of course a part of them knows none of it can possibly be true. They know how their world works and what we do here just doesn't fit so it must be faked…But what do they do? They play along, because a part of them wants to believe. To explore the unknown. They want to believe in the magic. And if everyone is pretending that it's real, who's to say it's not?"

I sat with her words.

"So your lesson today; Believe in the magic." She continued, as she got up. "Keep an open mind."

I looked about the room once more and out the glass window before getting up myself and following her out through a corridor behind the bar. After a 20 minute walk and a service elevator up, we exited from a well hidden door that brought us up to the cliff. I looked around, astonished.

"There was another way in? Why did we jump off the cliff? We could've gone this way the whole time!"

"If we had entered this way then we wouldn't have jumped off the cliff, and where's the fun in that?" Princess Hilola laughed, heading towards the helicopter.

The next day, we were lounging about on Santiago's yacht miles off the eastern shore. Santiago and I sunbathed out on the deck, glancing down at Farrah as she applied a generous amount of strawberry scented sunscreen on the back of Moncyra's thighs as she flipped through a tabloid magazine.

Santiago sighed. "Game well played, amigo."

I rolled my eyes and took a sip of my frosty bottle of Spanish beer.

"What are you talking about?" I sighed, knowing very well what he was talking about.

Santiago looked over at Princess Hilola, who was sprawled out on a white life raft being pulled beside the yacht. She stared drowsily into the tiny waves of the ocean, swirling her fingers over the water.

"She is…no ordinary woman, Kelley." Santiago said. "She requires more. More than the yachts, the acres, the inheritance."

I also watched Princess Hilola. Out of nowhere, the snout of a bottlenose dolphin appeared before her from the water. Without a moment's hesitation, she affectionately caressed it's head.

"You have something I cannot give her," he continued. "She's chosen you. I want to be remembered as dignified and graceful so naturally, I will back off. I leave tomorrow."

I, astonished by the Princess's interaction with a wild dolphin, could barely pay attention to Santiago's blathering, let alone follow it. After a moment it seemed as if the dolphin and the Princess came to an agreement of some sort before it sank deep below the waters and disappeared. I then casually glanced over at Santiago only to find him staring back at me with a look I'd never seen on his face before. He was dead serious; it nearly startled me.

"She wants your heart, Kelley." Santiago said, staring into my eyes. I stared back at him. Santiago's stern demeanor then melted into a jovial smile.

"Your pure heart." He continued, breaking his stare to survey the horizon and take a swig of his beer. "She's chosen you and there's absolutely nothing I can do. And even if I could do something, anything, to destroy you and win her affections…I wouldn't do such a thing."

We both looked back over at Princess Hilola; the dolphin had returned, carrying a blush pink perfectly intact lace murex shell in its mouth. We watched as the Princess reached her hand out towards the dolphin and it placed the shell in her palm before disappearing again into the ocean. Princess Hilola admired the shell, holding it up and allowing it to glow in the sun.

"I truly love her, you know." I found myself telling Santiago. Though I was shocked by my own confession, I didn't dare show it because I could feel Santiago examining me.

"I know. So do I, and that's why I'll be going back home tomorrow. Her happiness is more important than my own."

I shifted in Santiago's direction. "Santiago, you don't have to leave. I know there's been some tension but I really do enjoy your company. This is just silly talk. She's so high above me. I'm just along for the ride to be honest. I don't want something like this to ruin your holiday." I told him in a moment of honesty.

Santiago shook his head and chuckled before taking a large swig of beer.

"There's that heart. Pure fucking heart."

PART 12 - DYING IN THE PALACE.

Later that night, Princess Hilola and her crew were entering CLUB: JADE, a swanky metropolitan style bar in the middle of the jungle.

We entered the designated VIP area and immediately began making drinks when I heard my name wildly shouted at the entrance. I turned around and saw my old roommates Paulie, Keith, Fausto, César, and Edvin all simultaneously fighting the brick wall of a security guard to get into VIP.

"BOYS!!!" I shrieked, making Farrah and Moncyra flinch, nearly spilling their flutes of champagne.

"They're my guests this evening. Let them in." Princess Hilola called out over my shoulder.

The guys practically spilled through the security guard's fingers and rushed over to me, drowning me in what was the largest group hug I'd ever experienced. I was fighting back tears the entire time; I didn't realize until that moment how much I missed them.

"I can't believe you left without saying goodbye," Paulie barreled into me and wept from somewhere deep within my chest.

I squeezed Paulie's head a little tighter, but not too tight. "I know, and I apologize for that. I was kind of being forced out." I parted from Paulie and took a step back to look him over. He was tan and far more muscular than I remembered. Even possibly a bit taller.

"What's going on with you, muscle man? The job treats you well, I see." I squeezed his broad shoulders.

Paulie blushed a bit. "I'm doing ok."

"Ok? Mini Rambo here went and got himself promoted. He's Head Regulator of his quadrant," Edvin beamed on Paulie's behalf.

"Not just yet. I still have to perform a standardized test and a leadership aptitude test. I haven't even had my second interview with the Captain of Nature Control, guys." Paulie shook his head, smiling.

"Modesto." Fausto tussled Paulie's hair.

"What are you guys doing here tonight?" I asked, noticing their stylish club attire.

"I invited them out. You've been so cool with everything. I thought seeing your roommates would be a pleasant surprise." Princess Hilola walked up from behind me and leaned on my shoulder. "Everything is on me tonight guys. Have fun." She smiled seductively. I couldn't stop smiling as well, seeing her put on her persona for my old roommates, who'd been hanging on her every word since she joined us.

"Bruv, we gotta have words!" Keith growled at me the moment Princess Hilola was out of earshot.

We drank till we couldn't see straight. The spirit in the entire club was so light and fun loving. Even the snow queen Farrah thawed enough to laugh at Edvin's flirty jokes. Once the music began to take over, we paraded out onto the dancefloor and joined the other partygoers. I even surprised Princess Hilola with a choreographed dance I'd been practicing with Tegra. Princess Hilola knew the dance as well, but she wasn't expecting me to be her partner, which made it all the more thrilling.

Near the end of the night, everything seemed to be in slow motion. I was doing my best at thwarting Ronan (as he tended to get handsy when he was wasted) when I felt a steady pull at my shirt sleeve. I turned to see a dull faced Keith.

"Can we speak, man?" he asked.

I nodded and followed him through the dancefloor, down the hallway and out the backdoor exit. I put my head between my knees and let the cool sweet jungle breeze wash over me. Keith paced back and forth in the clearing. There was a roar of thunder somewhere in the distance.

"You gotta listen to me, Kelley." He stopped pacing and pulled me up to look in the eyes. "How drunk are you?"

Inches from Keith's face, I stared down at his round perfectly puckered lips. "Not that drunk."

Keith let go and took a few steps back. "Good, you need to hear this, mate. Truth is we knew you were still on the island. You're all everyone's been talking about. The new boy in Princess Hilola's crew. The *chosen one.*"

I wiped the cold sweat off my forehead and through my hair. "What are you trying to say?"

Keith sighed. "Kelley, they're calling you the sacrifice. You've been picked to live this life of luxury because they're going to…to kill you. You're the celebrated pig before the big luau, fam."

I heard the words, but they were distant and hollow as if I were hearing them from underwater. I shook my head and looked up at the swaying of the palm trees, trying to grasp what Keith had said. Before I could respond, Khamarri came out through the exit door holding a bottle of rum and two glasses. He was visibly drunk. The intensity in his eyes was ever present as he glared from me to Keith.

"What are you guys up to back here?" he asked curiously, handing us glasses. "It's gonna rain soon."

"We're just catching up," I spoke up.

"Yea, it's far too loud in there." Keith added.

Khamarri nodded. "This island? It's sinking, you know." He poured us both a full glass then took a sip straight from the bottle. "Yup. If the volcano doesn't erupt soon, the tectonic plates underneath the island will collapse and the ocean will wash in on us from all sides. Crazy, right? The absolute and the only thing that will save us…" He then pointed upwards at the massive shadowy mound, the silent volcano hovering over them. "…is King Kalbar."

He raised his bottle toward the volcano. "Long live the King. Your bidding is my will and whim." He bowed slightly and took a large swig of rum. I took a hard sip from my glass, my eyes also locked on the volcano. A flash of lightning cracked over the peak, illuminating the spiraling walkway up to the top, just for a moment.

"Oooh!" Khamarri feigned shivers, grinning at us.

Suddenly everyone else spilled out through the exit door. Farrah was wrapped around Edvin for stability and Paulie was covered in lipstick kisses the same shade of deep purple that Moncyra wore. Keith, Khamarri, and I followed them back inside to find Fausto and César behind the DJ booth, mixing and fading and scratching up a storm. The crowd cheered them on and danced wildly. Tegra was on the microphone singing and shouting Japanese into the sea of shirtless boys and girls moshing against the stage.

I drunkenly danced for what felt like hours until I felt myself being grabbed by the hand by someone, Edvin or Ronan, and led off the dancefloor. Then, I remembered being led up a flight of stairs and out into the cold pouring rain. I was shoved into the helicopter, still drunkenly trying to sing the lyrics of Tegra's club mix. I remembered waving down at Paulie as we ascended off the ground, then immediately being back in the palace, laughing as I sprawled out across the sofa. I watched Moncyra squeeze out of her soaking wet mini skirt before collapsing on a pile of pillows and blankets they had arranged in the middle of the floor. Farrah adjusted her bra.

"Are those my panties?" She drowsily asked as she propped her shoulders against the sofa's edge.

"Bitch," Moncyra murmured, her eyes closed and breath heavy as if she were simply talking in her sleep.

I found myself unbuckling and kicking off my own wet pants. I removed my shirt and threw it over Ronan's head but he, who had immediately stripped to his boxers earlier before passing out, was too far gone to notice. I was just about to doze off there on the couch when Tegra, clad in ruffled boyshorts and Khamarri's tank top, motioned me over to the floor. With a smile, I crawled off the couch and stalked over on hands and knees until I was nestled comfortably in the middle of their slumber pile. Tegra nuzzled into my chest as Khamarri wrapped his arm around my torso, and I exhaled a sigh of extreme content.

"You're so sweet, Kelley." Tegra purred. "You're so considerate, and chill, and…" She yawned quietly and so did I, until a roar of thunder caused us all to shift slightly.

"…and I'm going to miss you when you're gone."

DAY - 19 - BOWVIOLET SPACE SHUTTLE - 184 HOURS UNTIL EARTH LANDING

Rebecca's head was spinning. She could barely concentrate on her daily ship maintenance routine. All she could think of was her great grandfather and Princess Hilola and the island. And Monclair.

After slumber cycle, that was usually the time she found herself rushing to her great grandfather's chambers in hopes that he would pick up where he left off. Rebecca would jump from her chamber, shower, apply her radiation protective skin cream, and rinse her mouth with the ultraviolet mouthwash before speed walking to his cabin. She'd enter and would find him there, slowly making an effort at some form of elderly calisthenics. She'd then either bring him his breakfast or they'd walk together to the cafeteria. Sometimes he'd immediately continue on with the story there in his room with little to no hesitation, other times Rebecca would practically pull the details from his mind and sift through the small talk he'd make in between the thoughts.

Today they were sitting at the observation deck overlooking space while listening to some music. Rebecca poured her great grandfather a cup of hot green tea. He smiled, picked up the cup, and inhaled the ribbons of steam deep through his nose. She sat impatiently, waiting for him to speak.

Part 13 - Bad Omens

I dreamt I had just boarded the new Tiger rollercoaster. Grinning from ear to ear, I couldn't hide my excitement as it slowly started to make it's way up the towering first hill. It was when I made my way to the top when I realized that off in the distance past the twists and dips, the tracks spiraled up the volcano and directly into the mouth. Why hadn't I seen that before? Panic washed over me and I shrieked in horror as I descended at lightning speeds down the tracks. Through loops and spins, I could do nothing but wail as I waited for what lay ahead. Before I knew it, I was climbing the base of the volcano upwards higher and higher until I came to an abrupt halt just at the edge of the volcano's mouth. I stared into the massive black abyss, trembling. My heart pounded so hard in my rib cage it sent tremors to my ears. I didn't want to die. There was so much to live for! So much I wanted to do, like…

Like…

Nothing. I couldn't think of anything to live for.

The coaster clicked forward a few inches, and I shuddered.

Frantic, I tried to think of something to live for, but much like the massive mouth of the volcano, my brain was vast and empty.

"Well…" I sighed, my voice echoing. "Damn."

And just as I felt my body plunge forward into the volcano, I awoke, back in my bed.

Another dream I'd had that week was one where I was a guest on a 70s game show. Intern advisor Mark with the host. He had this glorious curly afro, bushy mustache, and he wore a dazzling blazer and tie that matched his short shorts perfectly. He confidently sauntered around the stage and played to the audience. I was then made to choose Door #1 or Door #2 for my prize. After some consideration, I chose Door #2. The audience applauded as Mark sashayed over and generously opened the door. Out walked a pink flamingo tiger the size of a sofa. My hair stood on end and a wave or terror flooded my body as the giant cat spotted me and slowly stalked towards me. The audience burst into cheers and applause as it reared back and pounced on me, sharp claws fully extended. That was when I woke up in a total daze. Echoes of the audience still audible in my head.

Jared from such vivid dreaming, I stumbled out of bed. There was a faint rancid smell in the air. I breathed through my mouth and after a shower, went off into the kitchen. There I encountered Moncyra, sprawled out on the kitchen counter, eating cherries from a bowl. The rotten smell was noticeably stronger. I involuntarily made a face of disgust, my nose scrunched up and brows furrowed.

"Look who's up and about," she playfully sneered. "Want some cherries?"

I nodded and grabbed a handful. "What's that smell?" I asked.

"It's sulfur dioxide. It's a bit annoying now, and it gets in everything, but by tomorrow you won't even smell it anymore." She popped a few cherries into her mouth. "It's from King Kalbar. He's awakened."

I watched the color in her eyes flicker slightly, as if they caught the light of something…but nothing moved.

After struggling to look away from her, I slowly made my way out to the balcony. Once outside, the smell of sulfur nearly caused me to double over. I covered my mouth and nose with my shirt and looked out over the ocean at the main island. There in plain sight, stood the volcano bellowing small mushroom clouds of smoke into the sky.

"It erupted sometime early this morning," Moncyra spoke inches from my ear, startling me. She leaned back into the doorway, her mouth and fingers stained red, from the cherries. "The Princess is waiting for you."

"But…How is that possible? Six months ago we were all dancing inside of it-"

"Him," she corrected, firmly.

"…him. I thought the volcano was fake…" I continued.

She pointed up to the growing darkness that spewed from the mouth of the volcano and shadowed the surrounding island. "That look fake to you?"

I looked on at the apparently real and now very active volcano, speechless.

"The Princess is waiting for you," Moncyra again.

From the helicopter, I watched the lightning bolts dance furiously through the plumes of black smoke and prayed we didn't get too close. The feeling of dread sank into my body and I felt ill. I was dropped off at Le Grande De La Reese, where I watched the helicopter quickly depart, before making my way towards the Tigerlily Tea Haus. As I walked through, I tried to politely greet the women working there, my old coworkers, but they merely smiled or ignored me completely while going on about their duties. After nobody made eye contact, I figured they were purposefully ignoring me. What had I done wrong? Out on the balcony, Princess Hilola sat, sipping her tea, staring out over the jungle. She didn't acknowledge me either at first, but when she finally looked over and welcomed me to join her, I was afraid of what would happen next.

She poured me a cup of tea and offered me one of the various pastries on her tea tray before finally speaking.

"Today two people nearly died due to shark attacks, one of the roller coasters got stuck in a tunnel for 3 hours, and there are at least 6 known missing person cases that have been filed after a jungle tour guide lost her entire tour group. It's barely 4 in the afternoon." She shook her head.

Admittedly I had noticed that there was a darker presence that had covered the island like a thunderstorm. The beaches weren't as bright and waters had become choppy. The jungle just seemed shrouded by a threatening presence that was almost poisonous. Everywhere you turned there were more carnivorous plants popping up; giant menacing venus flytraps and the acidic wells of the nepenthes plants wafting a toxic metallic scent through the air. Even in the parks, the morale was at an all time low. Everyone was in a bad mood and the crowds were turning on one another. Just the other day two families got into a big brawl over a bit of accidental shoving in one of the confectionary lines. Paradise Parks was no longer the happiest place on Earth.

"It's only going to get a lot worse if I don't do anything. I know what I have to do and there's no way of getting around it. Kelley, I have to go back."

"Go back, where?"

"I have to go back to the volcano soon." She spoke as if we were younger and she was being called home to complete her chores.

"I don't understand."

"King Kalbar, he's causing all the bad things, but it's not his fault, it's-" She stammered and tried to focus her thoughts, which I'd never seen her do before. "Everything will be ok once I return."

I still didn't fully understand, but I saw how hard it was for her to try to explain so I sat there in silence.

"But that's only part of what I wanted to tell you," she continued. "I wanted to tell you that you've done so well and I wanted to give you a gift. A farewell gift, before I go."

Princess Hilola and I locked eyes.

"I want you to be one of us, officially. Tegra, Moncyra, Ronan, Khamarri, me, and you. Kelley, I want you to live in the palace with us forever. How does that make you feel?"

My mind drifted off in a sense. I was quite sure I was having one of those out-of-body experiences I'd heard about because I became fully visibly aware of myself all of a sudden. I saw us sitting there at that moment. I saw the birthdays at the palace. I saw holidays at the parks. Several holidays. I saw myself sitting here on the balcony of the tea haus with the Princess many years from now. I just didn't know how I felt about all of it.

"Now, don't answer right at this moment." Princess Hilola held out her hand and grasped mine, which strangely anchored me back into himself. "Don't even put too much thought into it right now. You have 48 hours to make your decision. There will be a royal induction ceremony. It won't be easy. It's going to take a lot out of you, and it will be painful. If you refuse, I'll respect you and I'll still love you, Kelly. If you accept…"

Her eyes welled up, crystal clear pools forming above her eyeliner.

"You'd be a part of something so amazing. So amazing. What we do here. What I do here is truly a privilege and a gift, Kelley. And you'd be a part of that."

She wiped her eyes with her cloth napkin and returned her gaze back off into the distance "Anyway, that's all I wanted to say. Enjoy your day off. There's a chauffeur waiting downstairs that will take you wherever you want to go."

Without a word, I rose from the table and started to leave.

"Kelley?" She called, unflinching.

I stopped as if a land mine were buried beneath me. I turned my head slowly in her direction, hesitant to meet her eye. "Yes, Princess?"

"Be careful out there."

I quietly and quickly walked out from the balcony, past Massoud, and out of the Tea Haus. At my request, I was taken to Cobalt Quarters.

After knocking at my old apartment door, I was greeted by a red-eyed Edvin.

"Speak of the devil, and he will appear." He said, sarcastically.

I entered the room and almost immediately realized how uncharacteristically quiet it was. No music, no Portuguese. No laughter.

"What's wrong?" I asked, studying Edvin's face.

"César was fired this morning. He was in a fist fight at work with a coworker and they fired him." He slumped down into a seat at the dining room table.

"Fighting? Why was he fighting?" I spat, furiously. I could feel the blood rushing to my face. "That's so stupid. He knows better!"

"He was only defending you!" Edvin shot back, also now visibly hot in the face. "Kelley, you should hear the way people have been talking about you. Whenever something goes wrong, they blame you. Princess Hilola has to be sacrificed but she's hesitating because of you. Something about restoring the balance on this stupid island and everyone's obsessed with it. Now that the volcano has erupted, they want your blood. Yours or hers."

I could only let the words wash over me. The fact that people I didn't even know wanted me dead was at the bottom of my list of things to process at the moment.

"Where's Fausto?"

Edvin pointed with an open hand in the direction of César and Fausto's room. I slowly walked to the room and leaned against the open door frame. Inside I saw the room was completely trashed, and Fausto sat on the corner of the bed amongst piles of crumpled clothes and shredded paper everywhere. He never looked up. Just stared down at nothing in particular.

"I'm so sorry, Fausto," I finally whispered after a moment.

"It's not your fault," he mumbled back, his voice raspy and weak. "He was always the hot-headed one. So stupid. I remember one time when we were little, we were waiting to be picked in a game of fútbol. Growing up I was a bit bigger than him, and he, being tiny and… He was usually picked last or not at all. I remember this one day the captains were picking teams, and when he wasn't picked, I thought he'd sit at the sidelines like he usually did, but that day my brother walked right up to the captains and asked to play. They laughed at him. He asked again, and when one of the captains shoved him away, he head butted him in the chest and got us both kicked off the field." He chuckled and looked up at me, tears streaming down his cheeks.

"You've got to bring him back." He got up off the floor and stepped towards me. "You were on your way home and Princess Hilola intervened. Maybe she can do the same for César. Maybe you can convince her."

I took everything I had not to burst into tears as Fausto bowed his head into my chest.

"I don't know if the rumors are true. I don't know what powers you've been exposed to, but you have to try, Kelley. Please."

I couldn't speak. I could only nod as I put my hand on Fausto's head in an effort to comfort him. I saw Edvin in the corner of my eye, watching us.

"Where is César now?" I finally spoke, directing the question more toward Edvin.

"He's somewhere in the jungle," he muttered. "Paulie offered to hide him there for a few days, or at least as long as he could. We were figuring out how to contact you."

I nodded. "I love you guys. I'll ask."

"Obrigado. Te abençoe," Fausto muttered amongst his sniffles.

"Be strong." I clutched Fausto's shoulder. "Keep César alive and on this island for the next 48 hours." I then stepped away and walked towards the door. "I'll be back."

I stepped out into the sunlight, disoriented, and gone, in every sense of the word.

DAY - 21- BOWVIOLET SPACE SHUTTLE - 155 HOURS UNTIL EARTH LANDING

Sprawled out on the floor at the discretion of her captain's chambers, Rebecca stared at the ceiling and wept. It must've been a combination of exhaustion and early symptoms of space discomfort, she thought to herself. The tears streamed from her eyes and gathered to a pool around her ears as she allowed herself to wallow in what she could only describe as sadness. She thought of Monclair and that smirk she made right before she did something she wasn't supposed to, also how she handed the codes to her shuttle, despite being so angry with her. She thought of her friends back home, and how she missed them so much. So much. They weren't a large group, but they'd found each other out there and that meant something to her. She thought of her mother and the last time they'd expressed their love for one another without feeling obligated to. She thought of her great grandfather, and this wild story. She felt disconnected, and she wasn't quite sure why. It was just so much built up.

About an hour or so later, she rose up and wiped her face. She felt lighter, and somewhat foolish. Not ashamed. Foolish that the little things that seemed to make up a big internal mental problem dissolved and streamed from her eyes, one at a time.

PART 14 - PURE

48 hours later, I found myself getting ready to go out for the night. Dressed in head to toe white and dripping in gold jewelry, I was reminded of the first night I joined Princess Hilola and her gang. I was so unsure and so afraid. When I looked in the mirror, fixing my hair and repositioning my necklaces, I felt changed. In fact, I hardly recognized the guy I was eight months ago, much less felt like him. I walked to the roof and boarded the helicopter. A few minutes later, I arrived at what looked like a clearing in the jungle. There in the middle stood Tegra, Khamarri, Moncyra, Ronan, Farrah, and Princess Hilola. They stared at me emotionlessly and unflinchingly.

Princess Hilola spoke first. "I need an answer, Kelley. What are you willing to do?"

Before I spoke, I looked up at the jungle skyline, where the star lit night sky and swaying trees of the jungle connected. It was peaceful.

"I love you, all of you, so much. I think of you as the brothers and sister I never had and I love the time I've spent with you guys on this island, and to pack up and leave this behind, terrifies me. Back home, I have nothing. I am nothing. I've grown so much and learned so much about myself. I owe that to you, Princess Hilola, and any way I can repay you, I'm willing. I can't say no. Not to you."

Farrah and Tegra quietly fought back tears and fanned themselves while Hilola stepped up to me and embraced me.

"Thank you," she whispered into my chest just loud enough for me to hear.

I saw Ronan glaring at me, a look of annoyance on his face, but I also saw fear. I chose to ignore it.

"You're welcome."

"Ok. We can't waste any time." Khamarri cleared his throat. Hilola pulled away and looked into my eyes.

"Follow me," she said, and headed off, with everyone trailing behind her. Freshly broken glow sticks in hand, we stalked through the jungle and eventually entered what I wouldn't call a cave exactly, but an extremely old man-made tunnel etched into the hillside and shrouded by vines. We walked in silence through the tunnel for what felt like hours until Tegra looked over her shoulder at me and took my hand in hers.

"I'm so happy for you, Kelley," she beamed. "This is such an honor. You're finally a part of the club!"

"You guys all went through this?" I asked.

"Tonight will be my, what, 13th anniversary?" She yelled up ahead of her.

"Your 14th!" Moncyra replied. "My 21st."

"28th." Khamarri added.

"So fucking OLD!" Princess Hilola threw her head back and shrieked, causing the tunnel to shake violently, as if they were experiencing an earthquake, but it only lasted a few seconds. Everyone laughed. Everyone except me.

"Anyways," Tegra continued, casually. "This is a very auspicious moment in your life. I know you have no idea what's going-"

"No idea." I heard Ronan murmur.

"I understand," Tegra continued. "I've been there. But know that this is bigger than…than anything you can imagine. Believe that, Kelley. You're next level." She gripped my hand tightly as we reached the end of the tunnel. What I thought to be the sound of running water had gradually become a booming roar of cheering and drums. Tegra turned around fully towards me, grabbed my head, and we pressed foreheads together. We locked eyes and in them I saw something wild. It was the same flicker I'd noticed in Moncyra the day Kalbar erupted. Almost animalistic.

"You're going to die tonight," she whispered into my mouth with a grin before bounding off through the tunnel exit.

Before I could process, I was engulfed in the base of a giant coliseum ruined in vines and jungle growth. There were people in the stands applauding and dancing as musicians banged furiously on a row of drums. At the top of the coliseum sat Massoud, in his typical peach mint suit and icy demeure.

I then noticed Regina Hunama, sitting with Massoud. Her lips, saturated with a shiny red lipstick. She glared down at us, still and unmoving, statue-like. The red orchid in her hair had it's vines entangled within her high bun as if it had grown there, and confidently displayed itself, daring to be tampered with.

In between us was a megalith, heavily decorated with living flowers and candles. I couldn't make out the inscriptions from where I stood, but I felt that it was a shrine dedicated to Paradise Parks Founder Mr. Hunama himself.

I was led by Ronan and Khamarri to the center of the stadium and onto an old stone platform. There, I was brought to my knees before being bound and gagged. Princess Hilola silently watched on as Moncyra approached me brandishing a dagger. She pulled at the navel of my shirt and effortlessly sliced through it, cutting it from the nape of my neck down until it was completely split in two, allowing the remaining pieces to fall to my wrists. Bare chested and restrained, I could only look on as Farrah and Tegra anointed me with two different oils. The one used on my face smelled of rosewater and black tea, while the one used on my back gave the areas of contact an intense tingling sensation.

Eyes tearing from the fumes of the oils, I watched as Princess Hilola was adorned with long golden talons on each finger, a large peach colored fur shawl that glowed as she caressed it, and a massive red feathered headpiece that seemed to move and twitch on its own. I squeezed the tears from my eyes and shook my head as they painted her face.

The drums blared wildly as the creature once known as the Princess approached me. Her moves were now slow and tactical as if at my slightest move she would devour me whole or spread her wings and fly away. My eyes followed her as she neared. She stood a few feet in front of my face, but I barely recognized her. Her eyes were bloodshot and shiftly while her face was stone still. I could hear her breathing heavily through her flared nose. She leaned in closer and that was then that I noticed how much I was shaking in terror. This didn't feel fake or staged for the guests. I was realizing that this was very real.

Princess Hilola stuck out one of her long golden talons and slid it slowly down my trembling chest and stomach. She then pointed the talon over my heart and slowly pushed it beneath my skin. I wailed in pain, but it was muffled by the gag in my mouth. Princess Hilola removed the talon from inside my chest and theatrically examined the dark blood running down it. She smelled it, watched the blood trickle from my wound down my body, then brought her attention back to the blood on the talon. She smelled it once more before licking the talon clean. The crowd on the stands cheered and hollered as she did this.

She backed away as Ronan walked over and removed my gag, which made me dry heave and gasp for air. Then Khamarri walked over carrying a large bejeweled goblet of a smoking liquid much too dark for me to clearly recognize. Khamarri got down on one knee and gently handed her the goblet, which she clasped with both hands and slowly walked back towards me. She stood over me and lifted the cup over her head towards the starry skies. She then lowered it to my face and all I could smell was hibiscus and sulfur. And blood.

"Drink." I heard the Princess say, though when I looked up, I saw no evidence of her speaking. She just stared down at me, eyes wild and enraged.

I opened my lips slightly and the liquid came rushing in, filling my mouth and coursing down my throat. It was gritty and, despite its steam, lukewarm. My eyes welled up with tears as I tried to down the entire goblet, allowing much of the excess to pour down my neck to my chest. I gagged for air and tried to keep it all down. I looked up to find the slightest smile had spread across Princess Hilola's mouth. Her glare now giving me an intense sense of affection. This uncontrollable urge washed over me. I wanted her at that moment in ways that terrified me. I was so focused on getting to her, I didn't notice a large basin of fire had been set into place beside me.

I looked at her face, and saw warmth, love, and acceptance. I saw everything I'd ever wanted. I saw a reason to live.

Beside us Ronan was now stirring or stoking the fire with a long thick stick, causing embers to drift high into the air. I was now fixated on Ronan, and I jolted when Khamarri put the gag back on me and tightened the straps until it was tight against my cheeks.

I locked eyes again with Princess Hilola, who was still smiling slightly, though her eyes were now pooling with tears.

Frantic, I watched Khamarri pull the poker from the flames, exposing the ultraviolet white glowing tip.

Crying and choking, I made several desperate attempts to free myself and call for a stop, but it was no use. Khamarri was making his way behind me as I shook my head and pleaded with Princess Hilola in muffled high-pitched grunts and squeals. She merely stared directly into my eyes, smiling a dreadfully sad smile, tears streaming down her cheeks.

It was the initial contact shock that sent my body into convulsions. After that passed, the searing pain of feeling the poker carve its way intricately through my flesh. Screaming as loud and as hard as I could was the only thing I could do to counter the pain. I could feel myself fading in and out of consciousness. I prayed for unconsciousness, but I looked up and locked eyes with Princess Hilola and everything went clear. I screamed directly into her face. I screamed out of rage and anger and hurt. I bit into my gag and growled at her. I looked into her eyes and saw the reflection of a vicious beast. I closed my eyes and I saw my mother. I bowed my head and cried uncontrollably.

Everything had gone silent and still. I found myself there, somewhere, in the void. I wanted to open my eyes but something stopped me. I could no longer feel my body. Was I dead? I didn't feel dead. Not that I knew what that felt like exactly, but this felt…like waking up. Soon, I realized I was lying on my stomach. Then, slowly, my senses started to return. I could hear rumbling and low voices somewhere nearby, and the rush of cool air against my wet skin felt so good.

"I'm just saying I think we made a mistake is all." A male voice came from the darkness.

"Well, it wasn't your decision to make so why are you pressed?" A familiar female voice replied. I opened my eyes and after a slight haze of disorientation, I realized I seemed to be in the helicopter, surrounded by Princess Hilola and the rest of the gang.

"What has he done to deserve this?" Ronan barked. "Princess, he's no one important. Just one out of the millions of picture taking sock wearing pasty faced buffoons here to exploit the island and your legacy!"

"Listen to you, Christopher Columbus." Moncyra sneered.

"I am 100% Russian, fuck you very much," he sneered back.

"How dare you question the Princess!?" Farrah exploded. "After all we've been through, all you've seen, you manage to doubt her. Have you no respect?"

Ronan then began this whole tirade about me, but I was far too exhausted to subject myself to his bitterness, so I allowed myself to zone him out. I zoned them all out. This had just happened to me and all those self-centered shallow sacks could do is make the moment about them. Or maybe I was the one being selfish. I switched my focus and concentrated on the heat radiating from my back: I felt the cool air intensely and it hurt to move my shoulders. I vaguely remember what happened in the ceremony, but much of it was lost. My brain was good at blocking out the trauma. It was many months and several therapy sessions later until I could come to terms with my mother's death. For her to be there with me and my father, and then literally overnight, completely gone. For a long time I was unsure which was the dream; life before her death, or life after. But this wasn't about my mother; this felt different. Flashes of white light where memory should be. Then when I came into realization, I felt this weight lift off my body and mind. I was feeling such a cathartic release there at that moment.

I opened my eyes again only to find them still at each other's throats. I had just made up my mind to drift off to sleep when Princess Hilola shoved Ronan out of the open doorway of the helicopter. I involuntarily jolted at the sight, which sent a white lightning strike of pain through my body. He let out a wail that was almost immediately swallowed in silence, then he was gone. Fallen who knows how many feet down into the ocean. Or land. I couldn't tell. Everything went black. There were a few whimpers from Tegra, then silence. I allowed myself to pass out.

DAY - 28 - BOWVIOLET SPACE SHUTTLE - 90 HOURS UNTIL EARTH LANDING

"I don't like her very much." Rebecca mused aloud, lounging across the shuttle sofa throwing a small red ball into the air and catching it repeatedly.

"Don't like who?" Kelley asked, slowly twisting himself to scratch his side.

"Princess Hilola. She's kind of self-centered and childish."

"We *were* children. She was a princess at the age of 17."

"I know…" Rebecca shrugged. "I just wish she'd been more considerate. It was obvious from the moment you two met that she was going to use you."

Kelley leaned back and looked at her. "Excuse me?"

"You were the only intern in your place of work, you weren't exactly excelling in the world of tea, and you were from a small town with a lack of cultural exposure. Grandpa, you were singled out by these people."

Kelley looked at her for a moment, then off into the distance.

"Princess Hilola…Massoud…they were in on this." Rebecca continued. "You said so yourself you didn't expect to move into an apartment people were already living in, right? What if your roommates were also in on it from the beginning?"

Kelley, silent and unmoving, continued to avert his gaze. Rebecca stood up and began pacing, deep in thought.

"What if Massoud gave you that limoncello to lose, giving you the perfect reason to break your contract and hang with the Princess? Now not only does Princess Hilola look like your saviour, but she now gets to use you as her reason to not return to the volcano, causing further pandemonium on the island."

After a moment of silence, Kelley leaned over and after struggling for a bit to get to his feet, he straightened his back and sighed.

"Interesting perspective. I think we're done for now." He patted her on the head, and left the room.

Rebecca stood there by herself, trying to piece together what had just happened.

Day - 30 - Bowviolet Space Shuttle - 42 hours until Earth Landing

It was 48 hours before her great grandfather approached her. He first acted as if nothing had ever happened and, admittedly, Rebecca was too ashamed by her bluntness to approach him. That evening as she was plotting coordinates for a hospitable landing environment on Earth, Kelley shuffled into the control room and sat beside her. Together, they stared at a hologram of Earth's geographical surfaces.

"Shall we continue the story?" he asked casually.

"Before we start, I want to apologize for being critical of the details of your story." Rebecca told him. "I got ahead of you and ahead of myself. I apologize."

Kelley nodded with a smile. "No apologies necessary, Rebecca. You're a smart young woman, and hindsight is always 20/20, but this is a story from a young boy's perspective. He's living all of what you hear. He doesn't have the privilege of the outside view."

"Understood." Rebecca nodded. "So, just how much of this story is true?"

Kelley smiled. "I'll let you separate the fact from the fiction. Shall I continue?"

Rebecca settled into her seat. "Please."

Part 15 - Hilola + Kalbar 4 Ever

I winced as the nurse applied ointment to my back. It no longer hurt, but the nerves were still sensitive and sent a chill down my back when touched. A few weeks ago when I could barely move, this was waking up in heaven, but today it was different. Not only did I feel fine, but after several weeks of bedrest and rehabilitation within the confines of the palace, there was a beach party happening at Paradise Parks I had no intentions of missing. Mostly because I needed to get out and get back to some sense of normalcy, but also I wanted to show everyone on the island that I wasn't gone. I had not been defeated. I was tested and I passed.

I thanked the nurse and slowly got dressed, careful and well aware of my movement limitations. The loose fitting Hawaiian style button up barely touched my back, but clung to areas wet with ointment. After an hour-long helicopter ride, I arrived on the strip of white sand beaches, crowded with skin-clad interns gallivanting and grinding amongst the ocean surf. The summer was coming to a close and this was very much something of a graduation party. The pop heavy tropical bass pulsated against my chest as I made my way through the dancers towards the side stage, where Princess Hilola resided. She was reclining on a massive chaise lounge of bamboo and cushion, shielded by the sun underneath an umbrella of banana leaves and massive black sunglasses.

"Kelley, darling." Princess Hilola outstretched her arms towards me. I kissed her cheek, bypassing the mix of perfume surrounding her.

"How's the party going, love? Can I get you a drink?" I asked, pouring two cocktails.

"Is there a party going on?" she joked, taking the chalice offered to her. "I hadn't noticed."

Khamarri seemed to appear from out of nowhere and grabbed the drink out of her hand. "Is that for me?"

He took a sip.

"Princess, take it easy." He then turned to me, who was wide-eyed and startled. "Don't give her anything else."

As he looked me in the face, and began to register who he was talking to, his stern expression softened. "How are you?"

I glared at him, hurt. "I've been worse."

Khamarri scoffed a bit and rolled his eyes before throwing the chalice into the sand. Just like that, he was gone nearly as quickly as he appeared. Annoyed, I looked over at Princess Hilola for some sort of explanation, but she waved him away and continued to bask under the banana leaves.

"What the hell is his problem?" I asked.

"I'm on a very strict diet. Very strict." She shrugged and looked off towards the ocean. I was sure that her eyes were tearing up under her shades because her lips began to quiver. I nodded, took a sip, and wandered off without another word. To be honest, I found it somewhat difficult to be around Princess Hilola and her friends after being sacrificially branded. I resented her too, especially when she (and everyone for that matter) pretended like it never happened. It's not like I expected a welcoming party where I would be accepted or celebrated or anything. Just some acknowledgment of what I'd been through would have been more than enough.

Even a hug…would've been nice.

I walked farther along the beach past the more aggressive partiers towards where the interns were just enjoying their day off at the beach. There in the distance I recognized Keith walking out of the water onto the shore. He was dancing to the music and waving his arms out at Edvin, who was underneath an umbrella, vigorously applying sunscreen to his bony shoulders. A few feet away, he noticed César and Fausto shooting one another with water guns.

It hit me again how much I had missed my roommates.

Unable to find the words, I walked up to them in silence. When Keith turned to face me, I caught a moment of confusion in Keith's facial expression. It only lasted a heartbeat, but in that moment he didn't recognize me, and I realized how different I must've looked compared to when we first met. The next moment was immediately followed by screams and cheers from both Keith and Edvin, who had risen to his feet so fast he'd knocked the umbrella up out of the sand.

"Kelley, bruv, it's so good to see you! My family!" Keith beamed.

"We thought you'd gone. I thought I'd never see you again!" Edvin wrapped his arms around me in a tight embrace. I groaned in pain and pushed Edvin back as a hot sensation shot across my back.

Finally got that hug I wanted. I have to be more careful about what I wish for.

"I'm sorry." Edvin muttered, back away. Word had quickly spread that I was no longer the tagalong in Princess Hilola's close circle of friends. Everyone knew, either by rumor or truth, that I had earned my place amongst them and I paid in blood, sweat, and tears in the literal sense.

"No, you're fine. I've missed you. All of you guys." I managed a smile and tried to pretend it still didn't hurt.

Behind Edvin, I saw César standing patiently, tears streaming down his face.

"Thank you, Kelley." César put his hand on my head.

"I'm just glad you're still here, César," I replied.

"Ok Ok Ok!! Mushy shit aside." Keith broke us apart. "I wanna see this branding."

I unbuttoned my shirt and slowly lowered it down off my shoulders. The guys huddled behind me.

"Äcklig!" Edvin groaned, covering his mouth.

"That's mad gnarly, bruv." Keith shook his head, with a smile. "The moment it heals completely, it's gonna look so cool. You're so lucky she picked you, mate."

"Yea? Well the next Princess who wants to take a hot poker to human flesh is all yours, man." I put my shirt back on. "Where's Paulie?"

"You mean Asian Rambo? Homie got another promotion and moved out. He now has his own apartment on the Nature Control basecamp." Keith said.

"What? He moved out?"

"Technically you moved out first." Edvin blurted, pretending to concentrate on the sunscreen he was rubbing into his shoulder. I attempted to speak in my defense but César jumped in.

"You should see him, Kelley," César gushed. "If you thought he was bulking before, you'd barely recognize him now. He's a total hunk."

Fausto punched César in the shoulder.

Suddenly there was a horrific shriek some distance away, followed by a bellowing fog horn. We all turned to find mass hysteria over the beach. People were frantically swimming out of the ocean as a crowd began to form around something that had washed up on shore. My friends and I ran over and pushed passed to see what the commotion was. When I finally made my way to the front for a view, I dropped my cocktail onto my tennis shoes.

A guy no older than me, who actually looked a lot like me, lay on the beach in a puddle of his own blood. Not a yard away, lay a massive washed up shark, it's jaws bared and red as it gnashed at air. The lifeguard interns, on and off duty, swooped into action and now had a compression belt wrapped around the boy's upper thigh, just below the chewed out chunks of where half of his thigh used to be. His flesh, in hues of pink and dark purple, had been washed by the ocean water. His eyes were closed and he was breathing heavily, exhausted. It looked as if the boy swam into shore clutching his life in his hands with his attacker trailing behind in hot pursuit.

A girl beside me buried her head in her hands and cried while a group of interns cared for the boy until the ambulance arrived. I recognized one of the girls who'd arrived in a jeep alongside the ambulance as the one who hacked her way through the jungle the night of the volcano party many months ago. She was talking into a walkie talkie and surveying the scene with intensity until she locked eyes with me and a bright and bubbly demeanor washed over her.

"Kelley! Oh my God! Long time no see, stranger!" She beamed as she rushed to hug me. A familiar searing pain shot down my back as I winced a hello.

"Oh shit! My bad, Kelley. Paulie told me what happened. I'm sorry." She backed away and tucked a stray hair that escaped from her ponytail behind her ear. "It's Cassandra…from that night in the jungle?"

I nodded. "It's fine. I'm fine," taking a few deep breaths through the pain. "I remember you, Cassandra. How is Paulie? I haven't seen him in months."

"He's doing really well. I knew he would." She smiled in a way that made me notice it was more than a smile. Suddenly her face lit up again like an exploding firecracker. "Would you like to speak to him?!?"

I shook my head and stammered a bit, but before I could get a single word out, she was already on her walkie talkie.

"Nature Control - Jungle Base, This is FLYCATCHER - 4 in Sector 7B. Requesting to speak with Commander P. Over." She spoke intensely.

There was a moment of silence before it buzzed and a response came through in a familiar voice. "Commander P speaking, FLYCATCHER - 4. Requesting the status at Sector 7B. Over."

"Sector 7B is reaching stability. We had a level 4 bull shark attack. Civilian is in critical condition but will pull through. I've seen worse wounds." She shielded her eyes from the sun. "Listen, I have a special class civilian here requesting to have a word with you. Permission to transfer. Over."

Another moment of silence. "Umm, permission granted. Over?"

She handed the walkie to me with a smile. I pushed the red button and leaned into the receiver.

"Commander…Paulie? Paulie, is that you? It's Kelley. Your old roommate…Over."

"Kelley, my best friend! How are you man?!?" The walkie nearly jumped out of my hands from the booming vibration of Paulie's excitement. "Damn I've missed you! How's everything? I'm sorry to hear about what happened to you. We were invited to go but I didn't want to and from what I heard I'm glad I declined. But damn. You're damn brave. So, how have you been? Over."

Hearing his voice made me smile. "I've missed you too, Paulie. I'm good. Aside from this freak accident that just happened on the beach, everything is ok. Over."

"Yeah, that's the fourth attack this week. They're getting more aggressive and we don't exactly know why just yet. Everyone has their theories." Paulie sighed. "Hey I'm throwing an internship graduation party myself pretty soon. I'd love to see you there, man. You'll get the details as soon as I get it together. Over."

"I wouldn't miss it for the world. Over."

"Excellent. It's funny how life works out, Kelley. We were so afraid and unsure when we first got here. But we rolled with the punches and took nothing for granted, now look where we are…"

I looked up and saw the lush jungle edge swaying softly with the wind. Upward, I heard the echoes of large beasts and birds of paradise call out to one another amongst the mountain mist.

"It's beautiful." Paulie went on, as if he were right there. "This world we've created for ourselves is so unimaginable and yet so distinctly ours. We must take every possible advantage, Kelley. Seize every possible moment. Over."

I closed my eyes and inhaled deeply. I became aware of myself at that moment, and I was grateful. "Thank you, Paulie. I'll see you soon, ok? Take care, buddy. Over."

"I'll see you soon, my friend." Paulie responded. "Request to speak with FLYCATCHER - 4."

I returned the walkie.

"FLYCATCHER - 4 speaking." Cassandra responded.

"Hurry back for an extensive debriefing. Copy?"

Her cheeks turned fuchsia and though she tried hiding her smile with her hand, it was beaming through the spaces between her fingertips.

"Roger that." She purred before discreetly saying things I couldn't quite hear, and really didn't want to hear, so I turned back towards the beach.

The guy that survived the shark attack had been stabilized and was leaving in the ambulance for the hospital. Most of the party goers had cleared the area, but the friends of the shark attack victim were quickly becoming an angry beachside mob. One of the boys had a closed parcel and kept threatening to stab the shark, or he would have already if it weren't for the members of Nature Control's efforts to stop them.

"Stand aside!" I heard a familiar voice boom through the beach. I watched as Khamarri and Ronan — who was sporting remnants of a healing black eye, a busted lip, and his left arm in a cast — parted the crowd and headed toward the shark. Khamarri was holding a large jeweled dagger. Ronan followed closely behind with a small bamboo box adorned with flowers. Triggered, I began to feel my heart pound uncontrollably against my ribcage as they moved closer. Everyone backed away as they hovered over the beached shark. Khamarri kneeled down, rolled the shark over onto its stomach, and rubbed the layer of sand off to expose its white underbelly. He muttered something before thrusting the dagger into its belly. It flailed and gnashed as Khamarri pulled at the dagger; a stream of blood and water poured from the wound. Bystanders stood frozen as Khamarri inserted his entire arm into the shark. The sharks failing and chomping went on for ten more seconds before stopping completely. It was dead when Khamarri pulled his arm out, gripping what looked like a blood covered football.

The shark's heart.

Khamarri placed the heart inside the basket Ronan was carrying, and wiped the dark red slime off his arm.
"I really liked this shirt." He shook his head and walked off, with Ronan closely in tow, leaving everyone aghast. "Free drinks for everyone! Go! Drink. Gossip," he threw his words into the air as they made their way back down the shore.

Later that night, we were all lounging in the living area. I was drawing Papayago on Ronan's arm cast while he was asleep when there was a knock at the door. I got up to answer, but before I could the front door swung open and in marched four tall men in military uniform followed by Regina Hunama. She sauntered in wearing a silk black jumpsuit and her signature stilettos. They boomed on the hardwood floor as she walked past me, jolting Ronan awake.

"Good evening, Kelley. You look well. How's your back, darling?" She shaded. "Where's Hilola?"

Far too shocked by her direct presence to be offended by her comment, I simply said "Thank you."

"You're late! It's almost time and I have to be at a party later." Princess Hilola came running down the stairs and wrapped her arms around Regina, causing everyone in the room to flinch. Even Regina's guards looked at one another, not sure if this was allowed.

Regina was stiff as a wooden plank, only making an effort to pat the sides of Princess Hilola while trying her best to shrug her off. "I'm not late. I'm right on time. We've got five minutes."

Princess Hilola unhinged herself from Regina and together they walked into the kitchen. "Right. It was a gift from the western shore today. Hope you don't mind it being cold." She was waist deep in the fridge when she pulled out a tupperware container of something red and wet. Deep down, I already knew what it was.

"We've had worse. Let's get this over with, shall we?" Regina said as she grabbed a candle and a bottle of brown liquor off the table. She did her best to sound warm and optimistic, but it came off as tense and tired.

Just as they were making their way to the balcony, Khamarri came down the stairs. Tegra and Moncyra moved from the bar and sat beside me while Farrah sat on the floor. Khamarri stood still beside the soldiers, his arms folded and his stance wide and territorial.

"Mom will be back in a bit, kids," Regina called out to the living room full of people. "Watch cartoons, or something."

They walked out onto the balcony and shut the door behind them, leaving everyone in a steely silence. None of us spoke to one another, and the soldiers stared ahead, despite Tegra and Farrah's playfully seductive advances.

After a moment, there was a flash of white light through the balcony curtains and then I felt a slight vibration that I couldn't quite escape, no matter how hard I tried. It was like the whole sofa was shaking, but I felt it on the floor and in his fingers.

"You feel that too?" Tegra put her hand up towards me and caressed my bare forearm. Her fingertips pulsated rapidly against my skin. It was an almost electric hum I could feel coursing through me, from her, but into her as well.

"What is that?" I whispered, almost afraid to disrupt whatever was going on.

"Very old magic." she winked.

"We know you've noticed the strange things that happen at these parties. The flowers, the influence, the way the island communicates with her. It's certainly something…" Moncyra pulled at a lock of her hair, looking at it as if the word she was searching for was trapped in her curls. "…more."

I shook his head. "Wait, so is the story of Kalbar-"

"KING Kalbar." One of the guards abruptly corrected him.

"He speaks." Farrah smiled.

"King Kalbar, my apologies. Is all that history real?" I asked the room. I didn't receive an answer right away. Everyone just looked at one another or ignored me completely.

"It's best if you ask her that question yourself." Khamarri spoke up. "This whole island is talking behind our backs. I don't want it going on in this house." With that, he walked off into the kitchen.

"Why do you even care?" Ronan asked, turning his head to glare at me directly.

I shifted upwards in my seat and glared directly back at him. "I'm pretty sure I'm allowed to ask questions, Ronan. Pretty sure I'm allowed to care. What's the deal with you, man? You've been nasty towards me ever since I moved in and especially sour lately. The thing that pisses me off the most, RO-NAAN, is that I have no idea what I did. So let's go there."

"Then let's go there." Ronan stood and planted himself squarely in front of me. I in turn rose up and did the same.

The girls were in shock, but in a gossipy, fascinated sort of way. Farrah squeezed in between Tegra and Moncyra.

"The reason I'm pissed, KELL-EY, is because I was going to go play football for FIFA. Tegra, has a Masters in Neurology. Farrah and Moncyra are both polyglots and Khamarri gave up birthright and a kingdom. A literal kingdom! Kelley, as a sacrifice, we've given up so much. What have you given up? Who are you?"

I stood there in silence. I felt the glares of the room burn hot on my skin.

"I don't know, ok?" I said, defeatedly. "I came here trying to find out just who I was and ever since I've been here I feel like I've been getting farther and farther away from myself. Also I didn't ask for any of this, ok? I was picked just like all of you so I must be pretty damn important. Also, it's really none of your damn business now is it?"

Ronan sighed, "I know I haven't been the most welcoming…"

I scoffed loudly and folded my arms.

"…but that's because I see the potential in you, Kelley. You have your whole life ahead of you. You don't need this place to be great. Dedicating yourself to this island…it's a waste. It's a mistake I-"

"You're talking too much." Khamarri warned. Ronan swallowed hard and sat in silence, not speaking another word.

Stunned by Ronan's sudden softness, I walked over to an armchair on the other side of the room. "You all had these impressive lives and what are you doing now? Clubbing and sun bathing and making out with one another. You're doing nothing and-"

All three girls audibly gasped and Moncyra rose up from her seat. "Excuse you! Don't forget, you were HIRED here for a job, which you were fired from. You were then picked by Princess Hilola herself, when none of us wanted you here, and showed you our jobs. Our JOBS, Kelley. Don't think for a moment we're not working. Don't think for a moment we wanted this."

"Whatever," Kelley sunk into the sofa chair, staring at a small green spider crawling under the coffee table. "If you don't want this then why do you stay?"

"We all know what the real world is like," Tegra explained. "The stress, the broken dreams, the loss. None of those things exist here for us. This fantasy fairytale is real for me. So, you ask why I stay. Instead, ask me why I don't leave."

One of the soldiers audibly sighed, clearly annoyed with us. We all silently glared at him as he continued to look forward. I then returned my attention back to the spider. It hadn't moved.

Suddenly the balcony doors swung open and Princess Hilola and Regina entered. Their hands and mouths smeared in blood, they made a B-line towards the kitchen and wiped themselves off. After a moment they emerged, still wiping their faces with damp cloth napkins.

"That was a bit more intense than I'd anticipated." Princess Hilola entered the main hall. Her face slightly stained red.

"Still wanna be part of the gang?" Ronan hissed mockingly, eyes locked onto me and my clearly bewildered reaction.

"It was…I thought…" Regina stopped picking blood from under her fingernails and thought for a moment. "I don't know, I just thought it would get easier."

"Yeah. I know what you mean." Princess Hilola nodded. "So what do you wanna do now? We could have a few drinks and watch a movie, or we could go to the pool for a swim. You're not still hungry, are you? I've got some-"

"Actually I'm going to go." Regina interrupted, eyes glued to her phone. She made her way back to her guards. "I have a prior engagement I can still make if I leave now."

"But, I really wanted to spend some time with you. We rarely talk at these parties. I just wanted to-"

"I already told you. I've got to go. I'll see you before then, ok? Take care of yourself." Regina turned her back to Princess Hilola and allowed her guards to escort her out the front door.

Princess Hilola stood there in silence for a moment, while everyone around pretended that they didn't witness what just happened. I looked on as Princess Hilola, ashamed and embarrassed, wiped the remaining blood from her chin before walking off towards the stairs.

"Kelley, I'm so glad we cleared the air. I feel a lot better. Let's be friends, yeah?" Ronan breathed a big sigh of relief as he laid back on the floor against the sofa, looking over at me with a big smile.

"Of course," I murmured, wondering exactly which circle of hell I resided in.

A few nights later, I was prepping for a rainy night out with everyone when Princess Hilola entered the main hall. She was wearing shorts, a tank top, and no makeup.

"I'm not going out tonight," she stated flatly before curling up on the plush sofa.

Everyone just stood there in shock.

"But…but we have to go." Tegra stuttered. "This is Regina's Annual Gala."

"I'm well aware, Tegra."

"No, let's just go, Princess." Moncyra rushed to Princess Hilola's side. Her voice was weakening and cracking as she spoke. I noticed the heaviness that descended upon the room the way age withers a flower. "It'll be fine. You don't even have to get dressed up. It'll be fun I promise."

"No…" Princess Hilola whispered. "I'm very tired."

"Are you sure, Princess?" Khamarri asked, masking his pain and surprise.

"Yes." She looked up at him and smiled.

Ronan was weeping behind his hands at this point. "Princess, I know I've been trouble but I just care about us so much. All of us! Kelley is my brother and I love him even though sometimes I don't show it, but we've made up. I'm so sorry. I promise, I'll stop, just please come."

He fell at her side and rested his head on her thigh. She ran her fingers through his bleach blonde curls, comforting and cooing him as he sniffled in her lap.

"My love…" She purred. "My darling, I love you more than you can imagine. This is not your fault or doing. I need you guys to attend this party, send a message to the establishment, and above all else, just have fun. You guys deserve it more than anyone."

They all took a moment to collect themselves and with heavy heads, they made their way towards the stairs to the waiting helicopter on the roof, until Princess Hilola stopped them once more.

"Kelley? Stay behind for a bit? I'd like to talk to you." Princess Hilola asked sweetly, though everyone in the room knew this wasn't a question. I nodded goodbye to everyone, and after Ronan, still red and puffy eyed, affectionately patted me on the shoulder, and they were off.

I nervously turned around and found Princess Hilola gazing towards the balcony door. Almost through it. I sat beside her on the opposite side of the sofa.

"First, I want to apologize. This is all bigger than you and so complex and layered, and I dragged you into this at the worst possible moment. I think now is the time you know why. I want to tell you a story."

"Ok." I nodded.

"Ok, so many many-"

"Wait!" I interrupted. I grabbed a pillow and sat on the floor in front of her.

"Ready." I smiled, snuggling in.

Princess Hilola chuckled. "Great. Let's begin."

The Bitter Realities, as told by Princess Hilola

Many many years ago, on the young island of Hilola, there was a family by the birth name of Hunama. They were a poor family, but they had four large lemon trees in their backyard that produced some of the sweetest lemons on the entire island. So sweet that Ricardo Hunama would send his two daughters, Regina and Florencia, to the marketplace with two large pails of lemons, and they would come home at night with two empty pails having sold them all. One day at the market a cloaked woman buying lemons struck up a conversation with Regina and became so charmed by her polished demeanor and personality that she continued to come to the marketplace to talk with her. She introduced herself by the name of Barb and claimed to be a drifter from a neighboring village. She'd purchase a handful of lemons and spend the rest of the day asking Regina all types of questions. She'd even buy the girls whatever they'd want at the market. One night, Barb insisted on escorting the girls home and meeting their father, then suddenly they stopped seeing Barb at the marketplace for weeks. It was two months before they'd see her again, though they didn't expect the setting to be having tea with their father at breakfast one morning. Barb then revealed to the girls that she was actually Queen Hilola, and that she'd been scouring the vast island for a young girl worthy of her son Prince Kalbar. She'd been speaking with their father for weeks in hopes of arranging a marriage between Regina and Prince Kalbar. Regina, who had finished school and was considered the more responsible sister, enthusiastically agreed to meet the Prince. Florencia, who quit school to help her father, was against the idea, but ultimately knew that her sister had made up her mind. The day they met Prince Kalbar, Florencia was quite surprised to see how he was nothing like the way she'd pictured him to be. He was compassionate and thoughtful and even slightly awkward. Blinded by his title, Regina fawned over him and treated everything he said as if it were gold, but Florencia knew he was the type of boy Regina despised and never held in high regard. Being the closest female relative to Regina, she was to chaperone the courtship dates, where she would witness Regina grow more bored and frustrated with Prince Kalbar until she would excuse herself to be alone. This left Florencia and Prince Kalbar to discuss art and poetry and music and what life across the oceans must be like. Kalbar admired her fearlessness while she admired his imagination and adoration for his people. One day, they snuck away onto a bluff overlooking the ocean. It was there Prince Kalbar mustered the courage to confess his love for Florencia, but told her that he had no say in who he would marry and that he was under the mercy of his mother, the Queen. Florencia felt consumed with guilt, and even went out of her way to avoid him in future outings, but ultimately couldn't deny that she too had feelings for him. She'd never been in love, so she could not identify it exactly, but there was something in the way the Prince looked at her. Some bright glow in his eyes that made her forget everything she'd wanted in life, and suddenly, all she wanted was him. Florencia almost immediately went to confess to her sister, but after seeing how happy Regina was in planning her dream wedding, she kept silent. She knew Regina didn't love Prince Kalbar, and that it was an act on both their parts as they feigned affection in public. Regina's greed made Florencia's silence all the more deafening. The night that Prince Kalbar and Regina were to be married, Prince Kalbar fled to Florencia and insisted that the only way they both were to be happy was if they ran away and left the island together. Before she'd realized she'd said yes, they were running through the fields towards the departure docks. They waited on the sand all night for the boat to arrive. They talked, kissed, and held each other against the ocean winds. Finally at the break of daylight, Florencia woke to find Prince Kalbar staring at her. In his hand was a golden ring, encrusted with various jewels and gems. The top of the ring had a jagged protruding rose quartz stone. He asked her to marry him, and she said yes. They didn't notice the boat at the dock. They were so focused on one another, they didn't notice the royal guards approaching them on the beach. They were captured and brought back to the palace. Prince Kalbar bravely confessed his love for Florencia to his mother. Astonishingly enough, the Queen had taken the news well and proclaimed that the two would be married at the volcano that afternoon. Regina was inconsolable. She cursed their bloodline and disowned her sister before running off into the jungle. Florencia went to follow her but was ushered off into the palace where she was washed, groomed, and fitted for one of the Queen's dresses. Florencia was shaking and physically ill the entire time. She wanted none of this. She didn't care for the kingdom, or the title. All she wanted was to make things right with her sister, and to be with Kalbar. That was it. She was brought up to the cusp of the volcano, where Kalbar was waiting, dressed in white and gold. He looked like a God. His face was red and wet, as if he'd been crying, but Florencia was drawn to the smile on his face. It was all she could see as she joined him at the edge. The shaman who stood before them bound them in the ceremony. His jet black hair and tan leathery skin glowed above the bright molten lava that churned below them. He spoke of the sky and of the water, of space and the stars. After Kalbar slid the ring on her finger, they kissed. Her eyes were closed for only a moment, then she felt a forceful shove against her body. The Queen was pushing her, and it wasn't one swift push, but several long shoves and pushes. Florencia struggled to gain her footing, and grasped for Kalbar, but it was too late. She'd begun falling into the mouth of the volcano. She managed to let out a single shriek of horror before colliding with the bright molting lava. There was but a moment of pain, then complete blackness. Florencia ceased to exist…and then, she existed. She *knew* she had fingers, but she couldn't see or feel them. She tried to speak, but heard no words. In fact, she didn't hear anything at all. She was in the void, trapped in her own thoughts amongst the silence. Suddenly from within the darkness, Florencia noticed a very dim glow. A yellow orb of light, moving ever so slightly. It was floating at eye level and shifting shape. As the orb grew closer, Florencia felt warmer, like being embraced in a grandmother's hug. As it grew brighter she felt her body, and a sense of space. She was completely consumed by the white orb, which blinded her, causing her to shut her eyes tightly and raise a hand to shield her face. Suddenly she could feel a cool breeze come over her head and move down her body. She moved her hand and gazed out at the lush green jungles of the island. She had emerged from the mouth of the volcano. No longer Florencia, but Princess Hilola. She stepped down onto the warm volcanic rock, and fern grew beneath her feet, she stood before over a hundred people bowing before her. The only ones standing were the shaman, whom she recognized from the wedding, and Prince Kalbar, who was a much older man now. His greying hair visible underneath the crown his mother once wore. His face looked the exact same. She ran to embrace him and was engulfed in his arms. He felt like home, but off in the distance over his shoulder, she noticed a pair of eyes blaring out from the darkness of the jungle. The eyes, stark white all around with large black hollowed out pupils. The dark figure stalked through the edge of the clearing, just out of sight. Princess Hilola did not move, but followed it with her eyes. She watched the pair of eyes move up 10 feet into the trees, then down inches above the grass. The figure faded back further into the darkness until it disappeared completely. She knew it was her sister.

Part 16 - Dark & Sweet

A couple days later, I had closed myself away in my palace bedroom. Despite my best efforts and all the modern luxuries of a palace at a theme park could offer, depression found me, disguised as homesickness. I barely had the will to get out of bed, let alone participate in the shenanigans of a royal princess and her shallow friends. Quite simply, I was done.

My phone's music library had shuffled from sad song to sad song when I received a knock at the door.

"Come in." I groaned.

Two men dressed in full military regalia stepped in, causing me to shoot up in my bed. They stood at attention beside the doorway.

"Her Highness Regina Hunama requests your presence. Formal attire, please," the man with the large mustache said sternly.

"What? I don't…Where are we going?" I asked, dumbfounded.

"Sir, please. Get dressed." The other soldier said, his hair lip scar accentuated in his snarl.

I sat, frozen. All I could do was muster a couple words.

"N-No. I'm not going anywhere." I muttered.

The two soldiers stepped forward only once.

"We're not asking, Kelley."

Two hours later, I was dressed in a black cocktail tuxedo, at a desolate coffee shop called 'Dark & Sweet'. It was a small shop located just outside the Paradise Parks entrance. Shielding myself from the drizzling rain, I turned and tried to peer through the heavily shaded windows of the town car.

"I'm a little overdressed for an americano, guys. What am I doing here?"

The window cracked open about an inch. "Ask for the Kopi Luwak."

"The what?"

The car drove off, leaving me in the parking lot, in the rain.

When I entered the coffee shop, I was surprised to see that it was actually open. There weren't but four small round wooden tables, one of which two elderly men played dominoes while sipping Cuban coffees, and the barista sat on a stool at the register. He was engrossed in the book he was reading and didn't acknowledge me when I spoke for the first time.

"Hi, hello." I tried a second time, louder than natural.

He looked up innocently.

"Oh, I'm terribly sorry. What can I get for you?" He asked politely, the smallest curl of a smile across his lips.

"Can I please have…" I looked up at the menu behind the boy, searching for Kopi Luwak, but I didn't see it. "…um, can I get a Kopi Luwak?"

"I'm sorry?" The boy asked, a flash of confusion on his face.

I cleared my throat. "A Kopi Luwak."

The boy shook his head. "I'm terribly sorry. We don't serve that here. Would you like a latte, perhaps?"

"I was told there was Kopi Luwak here. I dunno. Are you sure you don't have any?" Slightly flustered, I asked again.

"I'm terribly sorry…" The boy shrugged and returned to his book.

"Thanks." I threw my hands up, defeated, and went to walk out of the shop.

"Young man."

I turned around towards the two old men playing dominos. One of the men waved me over and I stood over them as they played, the smell of cigar smoke and strong cologne filling my nostrils.

"You guys are getting younger and younger. Jose, look at his face. Your mom let you out this late?" The chubby balding man chuckled, teasing.

He placed one of his dominoes down while cupping the other perfectly in a row with the other hand.

"It's the preservatives, I'm tellin' ya." Jose shook his head. He hadn't bothered to look up at me since I'd been standing there. Instead his eyes were peering over his glasses, fixed on his own hand of dominoes.

The balding man closest to me looked up at my face with beady black eyes swallowed by a round sweaty face. "Are you over 21, kid?"

Slightly taken aback by the question but only for a moment, I adjusted my tuxedo coat. "Yes, I am."

The sweaty old man smiled and nodded. "Sure you are."

"Do me a favor, will you? Take his domino to the mechanic's room." Jose said, more to his hand than to me. He then grabbed one of the spare dominoes and handed it to me before returning to his game.

I gripped the domino and looked around the old coffee shop. After a moment I noticed a small hallway behind the barista's coffee making station.

"Hey, change your mind about that double espresso?" The barista asked, cheerfully.

"Actually," I started, matching the barista's demeanor. "Can you point me in the direction of the Mechanic's room?"

"Of course! It's past the restrooms, then the last door on the right."

"Thank you," I said, heading to the back hallway.

"Stay to the right," the barista then repeated curtly, darting his eyes at me just above his book.

I nodded and ducked off into the hallway in the corner. There, I passed the bathrooms, storage closet, and an unnamed door before stopping in front of a door on the right label in gold 'Mechanic's Room'. When I opened the door and entered, I realized it was just a small empty closet. When I walked inside, the door swung shut and the lights flickered for only a moment. I looked around, confused. Everything vibrated for a minute or so then a stillness came about the room. Then I heard a hollow thud from the other side of the door. I opened it to find myself not in the coffeeshop hallway, but a new room all together: a waiting room of sorts. There was music and laughter coming from behind the multilayer curtains of red chiffon.

Behind a seamless black marble desk sat a girl, head buried in a book she was reading, her strawberry blonde curls cascading over her shoulders.

"Hi. Excuse me…" I approached her desk.

It was when she looked up at me did I see that besides the hair and makeup, she was the spitting image of the coffee shop barista, in female form.

"Oh, I'm terribly sorry. How can I help you?" She asked, same curl of a smile, and same voice only a pitch higher.

Stunned only for a moment, I focused. "Yes…I'm here to speak to Regina."

"Of course. Domino, please."

I handed her the domino which she examined for a brief moment. "Right this way!" The girl put the book down and almost immediately the flowy curtains behind her began to lift and part. Once a path had shone itself, I followed her down the walkway.

I was led into a casino of card and dice tables. Large men in suits yelling in languages I couldn't understand through thick cigars. Servers wearing little to nothing slinked through the crowd while dancers arched and flexed on neon platform stages. The whole place reeked of tobacco and perfume and dark liquor and old money. I did my best to keep my eyes forward, ignoring the menacing glances I could feel, daring me to make eye contact.

We reached a private lounge booth area where I saw Ms. Regina Hunama perched before a black glass table. She was drinking from a teacup and jotting down notes into a small notebook with a feathered quill. Her raven hair finger waved impeccably around her signature blood red flower.

She looked up directly at me. "Hello Kelley! Please, have a seat. Join me." She said with no malice, or snide in her voice, but with a sense of warmth I did not expect.

I walked past one of her massive guards and climbed into the seat beside her.

"How are you enjoying your stay on the island?" she asked, putting away her notebook and quill.

"I'm having a great time." I feigned pleasantries.

"I'm sure." she smiled, studying my face for a moment before putting her focus on her tea. "I wanted to talk to you about everything. I'm sure she's spoken to you about all of this, but I couldn't let you go without saying my piece."

"Ok." I nodded.

"First I wanted to thank you for being there for her. I know it wasn't easy. And I can't imagine what you went through." She said, sincerely.

"I thought I was going to die, and to be quite honest, I was ready to die. I didn't have anything to live for before this place." I locked eyes with Regina, feeling at my most vulnerable, and had no idea why I would tell her such a thing once the words left my mouth.

"Sweetheart," She raised the cup to her lips, slightly masking the smallest smile. "You did die."

I looked at her as she took a dip from her tea cup. A flush of confusion washed over me.

"What?"

"Your heart stopped. She attempted to sacrifice you in an attempt to save herself. But it didn't work. Nothing changed."

My brain spinning, I searched for the words.

"But, she told me it was a ritual to make me a part of her group. She said I could stay forever."

Regina shook her head and vigorously stirred her tea. "Just like her. She thinks her lies are always sweeter than the truth, and I become the bad guy for telling it like it is." She said more to herself than me.

"The fact is what she said was half true. Your sacrifice would indeed bind you to her and her gang, but ultimately she has to give herself to King Kalbar in the closing ceremonies. She thinks if she manipulates the system and plays it to her liking, the results can change. Think of it as a puzzle. You, Khamarri, Ronan, the girls…myself included. She thinks she can rearrange the pieces and place them where they don't fit, but it doesn't change the picture."

I sat in silence.

"…Do you want me to explain further?" She asked, in a daring tone.

I felt a swell in my chest. I looked at Regina and shrugged. "No. If it's done, it's done. I accepted this place for what I thought it was and as I peel back the layers I'm beginning to realize that the more I fight the less control I have. I just want to know, why have you chosen to tell me this now?"

"Because I believe in transparency. I believe in alchemy, not magic. I also believe your ignorance won't save you from inevitable outcomes. Knowledge really is power. Ignorance is not bliss. You know…" Regina hesitated for a moment. "…you could've walked away at any time. Even if we didn't make it feel like you could, you always had that option. You still do."

"Thank you for telling me, Princess Regina." I smiled. I didn't mean to sound sarcastic, but it couldn't be helped, and I found it all almost funny.

Regina looked down far enough at her cup as to hide her face, but I could still see the subtle joy on her face.

"I wish you nothing but the best, Kelley."

Her guards parted and I knew that was my cue to leave. As I gained a couple feet away in the distance I heard her voice call behind my shoulder. It was clear, and stern, but I could almost see the playful smirk in her voice.

"Don't get lost…again."

I laughed. Hilarious.

Day - 31 - Bowviolet Space Shuttle - 21 hours until Earth Landing

Rebecca surveyed the scene as the Bowviolet entered Earth's orbit. There was so much orbital debris surrounding the atmosphere, finding a large enough window to enter in the proper time frame while attempting to steer clear of it all would be difficult.

She pulled up a 3-dimensional geometric map of the planet and studied the debris' rotating patterns. She studied the surface density. She studied the oxygen levels and air quality. The odds were slightly against her, but landing wasn't impossible. She had to get to Earth, for her great grandfather. To be quite honest, the story he'd been telling her for the duration of the trip was the most fabricated, most extravagant story she'd ever heard. She didn't believe most of it, but she wanted to. It was the way he told her the story. The way his eyes came to life as he heard his own words echo in the hollow chambers of the ship. That was by far her favorite part of the story. She wanted to get to Earth and make his eyes light up like they did when he told his story.

Rebecca heard slow shuffling footsteps approaching from behind. Without reacting, she allowed her great grandfather to come in and hover over her. He'd become more interested in the landing mission the closer they came and the further he'd gotten into his story.

"How are we looking, Becky?"

"Ugh, not Becky." Rebecca involuntarily shuddered. She couldn't help it.

"Anyway, if we approach this from the Eastern Hemisphere at the arc of Earth's daily lunar calendar, we should be able to enter the atmosphere this time…tomorrow." She nodded.

"There." Kelley pointed to a spot on the globe. Rebecca squinted.

"There, what?" She asked.

"Can we land there?" He asked. "I'm not quite sure why, but can we land there?"

Rebecca turned around and looked at him, waiting for a more appropriate, more detailed explanation. After a moment she realized it was never coming, so she shrugged and turned her gaze on the globe.

"That spot there." She muttered. "Fine. I'll see if I can swing it."

Kelley patted her on the shoulder. "It's storytime." And he was off back towards the observation deck.

After a long sigh, she set the coordinates into the navigation system. She then got up and joined her great grandfather, leaving a pulsating red dot on the globe.

Part 17 - The Garden

The day had been entirely too muggy for the jungle, and entirely too hot for the beach. Once the sun went down, Paradise Parks began to vibrate with life and electricity. I watched, as I had many nights, the mesmerizing allure of the fireworks and searchlights dance around Paradise Parks from the palace balcony.

"Kelley, oh Kelley! Where art thou, dearest Kelley?" chimed a familiar voice from behind me.

I turned and saw Tegra leaning dramatically against the balcony entrance. She was wearing a frilly white cocktail dress and angel wings, which made me smile as I understood the reference. Her makeup was not yet done and her hair was still wrapped in curlers.

"There you are." She gave me a warm smile. "What are you up to?"

I sighed. "Nothing. Just…catching my breath, I guess."

"I know the feeling." She walked over and stood beside me. We glanced out over the horizon for a moment, silence broken only by the occasional burst of fireworks.

"So what will happen in the off season?" I asked. "What happens when all the tourists go home and we are left alone with all this?"

Tegra looked off somewhere in thought. "Life just sort of stops. Not in, like, some crazy we're-all-animatronics kind of way. How freaky would that be? I mean there's just nothing to do. The park shortens its hours, various shops close for the season, and we become pretty useless, for lack of a better word. All the parties and boating trips are only available when somebody pays for them."

She smoothed out her dress with her hands.

"Even this get up I'm wearing. It goes back to the costume department after I'm done wearing it. A Lot of this…isn't as real as you think. I thought you'd realize that at some point." She looked at him and I saw a look of sympathy. I moved my attention back towards the fireworks and tried not to look hurt.

"Oh!" She snapped, "Princess Hilola would like to see you. I completely blanked! The helicopter is ready when you are."

She giggled in ditzy fashion and retreated back into the mansion.

When I boarded the helicopter and made my way across the ocean, I realized we were landing on a part of the island I hadn't been to before; it was a desolate cove tightly surrounded by mountains and far from the park and resorts. We landed on a flat cliffside clearing not far from the cove. I could make out a small bonfire on the beach as I let my adjusted eyes lead me through the moonlit path down the mountainside.

When I reached the beach, I found Princess Hilola stoking the fire. She wore a sheer white bikini cover up that matched my button down. She gazed on as the fire embers flew off the flames up into the air. She looked so peaceful, I almost didn't want to interrupt her.

"Where are we?" I asked softly.

She smiled, not taking her eyes off the fire.

"The island is sinking," she said aloud. "This cove was actually a crater. Rich in minerals with fertile soil, this was my father's first lemon orchard."

She then walked past the bonfire and towards the beach, stopping where the waves washed over her bare feet.

"Come closer, " she whispered.

I kicked off my shoes and socks and joined her at the shoreline. The milky blue water was warm and gentle as it washed over my feet and rushed back into the cove. I grounded myself in the white sand, and looked at Princess Hilola. She did the same and there, under the moonlight, I saw flashes of sadness shroud her features.

"I'm so sorry. For everything you've gone through." She said this quietly. "I've been so selfish. I've thrust you in situations you had no business in and I've asked a lot of you when I had no right to. I sincerely apologize for that, but I wanted you to know it wasn't all for nothing. Thanks to you, I get another chance. I get to come back."

My head was a hurricane of uncertainty, as was my heart, but I forced myself to speak before I thought too hard for too long.

"Princess, I trusted you. I thought you saw something in me, and accepted that. But I found out you were just using me the whole time. How could I have been so stupid?"

She stood motionless and listened to me speak. She made no effort in interrupting me, so I continued.

"I'm heartbroken, but I'm so grateful. I have learned so much about myself and I've learned that this actually has very little to do with you. It's about me and how I move forward. I've had the summer of my life. I wouldn't change a thing, Princess."

She smiled. "Follow me, please."

We then walked deeper into the cove, allowing the water to reach our waistlines.

"When this orchard started to flood, we thought we would lose the lemons…," she told me as we waded through the beach waters, her arms raised and outstretched over the ripples. She then plunged both arms deep underneath the water. I watched from a few steps behind her, perplexed.

"Then one day, a good day, my sister and I went for a swim…" She grunted uncharacteristically, thrashing with whatever was underneath. "…and we discovered these!"

She lifted her arms out of the water and up over her head. In each of her hands were two of the largest, roundest, brightest lemons. They almost glowed in the darkness. She turned and walked back towards me.

"Extend your hands," she softly demanded.

The very moment she placed the lemons in my hands, I felt a surge of vibrating energy flow from my palms, pass my arms, reverberate in my chest, and simultaneously up to my scalp and down to my toes. My ears popped and I got wave after wave of goosebumps.

"What…what is this?"

"Life. It's pure life."

She enveloped his hands into her own.

"Some call it Chi, or Ki, or Prana. The vibrational raw energy coming from these lemons. It's what made my father so wealthy. Nowhere in the world can life be plucked this way, and spread all over the world."

She leaned in, her eyes electric with wonder.

"Kelley, what if I told you everything we've ever needed; every cure, every elixir, the fountain of youth itself. What if I told you it was all put here on Earth and all we have to do is discover it?"

My heart was pounding.

"I…I would say that my whole life so far has been a waste." The words spilled from my mouth. Hot tears began to form in my eyes and I couldn't stop them.

Very slowly, Princess Hilola stretched her hands upwards and wrapped her fingers around my face. My tears fell into the ocean as she pulled me closer and kissed the center of my forehead. Her lips were cold.

"Kelley, by simply living your life, you've made it so valuable. Every time you make a friend, or learn something new, or fall in love, you become part of that equation. You become a cure."

She wiped the tears from my face.

"Thank you, Hilola."

"Thank YOU, Kelley."

I lifted the lemon up to my nose and inhaled deeply before offering it back to the Princess.

"This one belongs to you. Consider it a parting gift." She smiled, and walked past me towards the shore.

PART 18 - THE GRADUATION

I flushed my vomit down the toilet and brought large handfuls of water to my face from the basin bathroom sink. I wasn't hungover, but my nerves made my stomach very uneasy.

I looked up at my reflection in the mirror, and took in my current appearance. I looked older. Less shiny. No, not less shiny. I just shined differently.

Flashbacks of last night came racing through my head: Golden chalices, running on the beach, secret kisses in the jungle, dancing, shooting stars…

A tearful toast to Princess Hilola's last night.

I got dressed alone in the silence of the empty mansion that afternoon. Everyone had already left for the big ceremony at dusk. If I understood correctly, Princess Hilola would be sacrificed to the volcano in the same extravagant way she appeared from it.

I wasn't entirely sure what was real and what was for show at this point, so I stopped asking questions. I wasn't sure if she'd be gone for good, or if my so-called bond would bring her back. All I knew was I had the scars on my back. I knew they were real. They were the real proof.

When I arrived at the fairgrounds at the base of the volcano, festivities were in full swing. Many of the island guests were dancing about drunkenly and the end of days style debauchery seemed only heightened by the presence of children. I was watching two children viciously fight one another while their parents mindlessly sipped drinks when I was bumped by a girl sweeping trash into a dustbin. She tripped in an effort not to knock me over and ended up falling herself. Apologizing, I helped her get to her feet and realized that I'd seen her before. Her round face and curly red hair.

We boarded the boat to Paradise Parks together on the first day.

I tried to smile and say hello, but before I could say anything she was backing away from me, terrified.

"I'm so sorry for bumping into you, sir," she stammered nervously, her eyes darting everywhere but my face. She was pale and looked as if she hadn't slept in weeks. "Enjoy the park!" She shuffled off without another word, leaving me speechless.

Just then a booming horn echoed through the air from behind the crowd. Approaching the festival grounds from the ocean shore came a procession of people marching barefoot towards the volcano. A girl holding a large animal horn trumpet walked ahead, followed by a band of drummers, then a large crowd of over 300 people. They were draped head to toe in black fabric and adorned in what looked like ivory trinkets as they marched and swayed and thrashed violently in unison to the beat of the music. As they drew closer, I recognized Moncyra, Farrah, and Tegra near the beginning of the procession, flailing wildly and dancing swiftly through and around one another. Behind them stood Khamarri and Ronan. Shirtless and wearing black harem pants, they were the front pallbearers to a massive palanquin covered in sheer white organza. Inside was a small female figure kneeling down in a prayer's position with her hands in her lap and her head down. I assumed, but as the palanquin passed I knew without a doubt, Princess Hilola sat peacefully inside. She was a grenade that had not detonated yet, and she was a grenade that detonated a long time ago. I stood still and watched as the procession steadily made its way through the grounds and up the volcano.

The sunset had gone golden pink by the time they'd reached the top of the volcano. The band parted and allowed the dancers and the palanquin to come through to the edge. The dancers surged around the cusp until they were evenly around the volcano's opening. Khamarri and Ronan slowly rested the palanquin on the ground. Princess Hilola emerged slowly out the seat and the organza became her bridal veil. She stood still as the high winds pushed against her. All was completely still and the sound of the drums and the ocean were the only things that could be heard. The girls surrounding the volcano kneeled, then the boys holding the palanquin bowed at her feet, and everyone in the massive procession slowly bowed too, row after row, down the volcano. When it reached the grounds, I felt my body kneel down. I heard the snickers and felt the stares of the guests, but I didn't care. I could barely breathe.

Princess Hilola walked the rim of the volcano, grazing her fingertips across the girls as she passed. They were openly weeping now, as were Khamarri and Ronan. The tears streamed down my face, too. I couldn't stop them. I didn't want to.

As it grew darker, a warm glow from within the volcano's mouth became increasingly visible. The wind picked up and the sand beneath me shifted as I watched on. Princess Hilola looked as if she were glowing, too, as the lava's glow reflected off her white dress and wet skin. Suddenly, she'd taken her first step into the mouth, and there was a collective gasp among the crowd. She did not sink, as physics would suggest; instead she floated. Her feet were hidden somewhere in the steam and heat waves, and she glided to the center of the mouth. She surveyed the dark rustling jungle and spun towards her island home, then spun toward the ocean, then back. She spun, faster and faster, allowing her arms to outstretch and her head to tilt back. The steam kicking up and spinning around her while drums and wind intensified created such a spectacle. The tremors from the ground were so intense that many people had to brace themselves to find steady ground. Then, as if it couldn't get any more impressive, massive lightning bolts exploded and grooved through the volcanic plume she'd created. This inspired wild hollering and applause from the fairgrounds. I just kneeled there in awe. The volcano was erupting right before my eyes. Each element was a part of this massive orchestra, and she was the maestro. The grand conductor of a natural disaster.

Suddenly she halted mid-spin and faced the crowd. She looked down at us, and locked eyes directly with me. I could see she'd been crying, even from the distance between us.

"I love you." I whispered, my lips trembling uncontrollably.

She smiled and mouthed something. I couldn't make out what her lips were saying. I stood and wiped the tears from my eyes to get a better view, but they immediately pooled and blurred my vision. She kissed her hand and waved gracefully at the cheering crowd, and then a blinding orange light burst from the volcano and shot hundreds of miles into the night sky, consuming her completely. I winced, shutting my eyes.

DAY - 31 - BOWVIOLET SPACE SHUTTLE - 9 HOURS UNTIL EARTH LANDING

As the Bowviolet picked up speed entering the Earth's atmosphere, it went from dark grey to stark white. Rebecca monitored the shock levels. There were streaks of white and bright gold gaseous flames coming from the zones that permitted thermal soaking.

"Samuel, what are the RCC climate stats?" she asked urgently into the intercom system, not taking her eyes off the fire-glazed window shield.

"RCC climate stats are high, but expectedly so." Samuel replied.

Rebecca nodded.

In just under an hour, they would be in an oxygen rich atmosphere. Rebecca made a note to decrease the use of biofuels and oxygen reserve while increasing their solar intake upon their entry.

She checked the levels of gravitational pull.

She looked over at her great grandfather, who was standing still, eyes fixed on the streaks of flames licking the window. The flames illuminating the stream of tears rolling down his cheeks.

Rebecca made a note of comforting him after checking the atmospheric pressure. Immediately after.

PART 19 - ESCAPE FROM PARADISE PARKS & RESORT

It was over. Just like that. I opened my eyes to the applause of the crowd and a sulphuric mist swirling through the night sky. The tribal procession had vanished, the rustling and vibrating had ceased, and the volcano that was extremely active moments ago now looked like nothing more than a silent mountain, sleeping in the darkness. There was suddenly a rustle of commotion on the far end of the fairgrounds near the jungle. I turned and looked over towards what was going on from where I was standing.

"Something just grabbed him!" I heard a lady shout. There were people backing away from the edges of the jungle, while some were frantically running. Then there was a scream from the opposite end of the fairground. That's when I peered in at the edge of the jungle and saw a large black mass move through the bushes, just out of full view. I stood paralyzed in fear, eyes watching this figure move around us, passing another larger figure, then stopping to retrace its steps.

We were surrounded.

Then there was a shot that went off followed by the boom and glow of a firework in the sky. Frightened, everyone turned to see the bright red bloom. We were all momentarily distracted just long enough for a large animal the size of a compact car to crash through the jungle barrier and latch its jaws into a middle aged man mere yards from me and drag him back before he could make a sound. The surrounding crowd of people shrieked and mass panic had officially set in. The only thing I really got a good look at was a long tail covered in neon pink fur flickering out of sight. I shook my head a bit, trying to make sure of what I saw was actually what I saw. Then came a low growl of an animal just ahead of me.

We were surrounded by a pack of Flamingo Tigers.

Just as another firework went off, I lunged back, burying myself deeper into the crowd. I watched as a giant tiger darted out of the jungle mere feet from where I was standing. It roared and rammed itself into a woman nearby. As she clambered to get to her feet, the tiger sank its jaws and a massive claw right into her thigh. Immediately afterward, another tiger at the side of the grounds had emerged and was charging directly into the crowd, causing everyone to disperse into mass hysteria.

I darted down behind a nearby popcorn stand and quickly surveyed the scene. Thankful for the full moon and now continuous firework show, I was able to count four large tigers causing havoc around the camp grounds. They were maiming guests and getting into the concession stands. One had knocked over a corndog fryer and the grease almost immediately set ablaze to a wall of stuffed animals as it crashed to the ground. My chest heaved as I leaned against the popcorn machine. My only options were to run further onto the beach towards the ocean, or find better shelter. First, I needed to arm myself. My eyes darted around the grounds for anything long or sharp, and that's when I spotted the wooden mallet on the floor halfway across the room. It was from the high striker game nearby. I lifted himself up slightly to get where I could see the location of the tigers without them seeing me. Two of them were in a tug-of-war fight over a stuffed animal, while the third tiger was busy licking blood off its paws. I scanned the grounds, but couldn't find the fourth tiger. I turned and leaned back against the popcorn machine, and that's when I spotted it. Only a few yards away, it had found the roast pig concession stand and had the carcass nestled under its massive paws, gnawing on the pig's hind legs. I involuntarily gasped when I saw the tiger, causing it to look up and directly at me. It's eyes were small and beady, but it looked at me and I could see it deciding whether it should kill me or continue eating. Frozen, I sat there for what felt like hours before the tiger lowered its head and continued on with its meal. Feeling like I was finally allowed to breathe, I panted as I thought of a plan. I shot my eyes over towards the mallet and compared distances between the mallet and the tiger. I made note of anything obstructing my path. I made note of the toy duck pond and wall of stuffed animal prizes between me and the tiger, but I doubted that it would stop it. I looked at the mallet again. I was going to do it. This or be found by the other hungrier tigers.

Without flinching I jumped to my feet and sprinted towards the mallet. As if it had read my mind, the tiger jumped from the roasted pig and bounded in my direction. It jumped over the toy duck pond and crashed through the stuffed animal wall only to be met with a forceful blow to the face by me holding the mallet. The tiger fell flat to the floor struggling to gain consciousness. By this time the other three were attempting to corner me. They hissed and roared as I swung and prodded the mallet in their direction, all the while slowly getting closer. I backed up as well. Maybe I could make it to the ocean. Cats were afraid of water, right?

Just then a row of shots exploded onto the grounds between me and the beasts, flinging us both back. It wasn't until just then when I realized the flicking pressure of the helicopter above me, which was now shining a spotlight down as it lowered down a rope. I was about to climb the rope but instead saw a large dark figure latch onto the rope and propelling themselves down. The moment this man touched the ground, a tiger lunged directly at him. The guy pulled a black baton from his utility belt and jammed it into the tiger's gaping mouth. He wrestled with it only for a second before blue jolts shot from the ends of the baton and directly into the tiger's jaws. It jolted violently and fell back. The guy turned his head back and smiled at me. Something about his face looked familiar.

"Just can't stay out of trouble, can you, Kelley?" Paulie joked. He then flicked the baton and it extended into a double sided taser pole.

My jaw dropped. By the time I realized that the muscle ripped action hero that just jumped from a helicopter was Paulie, he was already off running toward an angry eight foot tall wild tiger. Paulie looked like he'd lost 60 pounds and gained it all back in solid muscle.

I watched in astonishment as Paulie grappled with a tiger and beat it unconscious. Just as another went to attack him from behind, a black jeep blasting music tore through the jungle and rammed the tiger clear across the fairgrounds. The jeep came to a screeching halt and Cassandra raised up from the driver's seat through the open roof.

"You boys need a lift?" She grinned.

"You're the absolute best." Paulie climbed up the side of the Jeep and gave her a kiss.

I assumed I'd wake up at any moment now because this all had to be a dream.

"Ahem!" came a voice from behind me. I turned to find a row of men and women clad in the same black and green cargo uniform as Paulie. They stood militantly.

"Right." Paulie hopped off the jeep and straightened his posture. "Squadron! Your primary is to tend and stabilize the wounded, then evacuate the survivors, and lastly to secure the area. We know how these animals work. Let's get these kitties back to their territory."

He leaned down and affectionately patted a tiger he had just knocked out cold. The animal purred in its sleep.

"Ok, Move out!"

And like that, they were put into action.

I walked up to Paulie and we embraced in a hug.

"Um…It's so good to see you." I shook my head in utter disbelief.

"I've missed you so much. I think I mention you everyday." Paulie said, grinning widely.

"Every single day," Cassandra reiterated.

Paulie turned red. "Anyway, let's get you out of here. I'm throwing that graduation party at my bungalow tonight."

"Yeah, I was heading there then all of…this happened," I lied.

"Cool. We were getting ready when we received the call. It's always something with this island." Paulie shrugged. "Cassandra can drop you off at my place. I got paperwork to file, then I'll be over to join in on the festivities."

"Ok." I hopped into the passenger seat. Still in shock and processing what just went down, I waved goodbye as we drove off into the jungle.

"Are you sad that the internship is over?" I asked Cassandra.

"Yeah, a little bit. Only because most of my friends are going back home. Paulie and I…We were both asked to stay, to work on the island full time."

"And he agreed?" I asked, surprised.

"They asked him first! He's the one who convinced ME to stay. He loves it here. He's not that little nervous boy I met in the jungle so many months ago." Cassandra said, her smile shining through the darkness. "He's much more than that now."

We eventually reached a paved road and stopped in front of a tree house style bungalow home that was booming with music and surrounded by partygoers.

I quietly groaned to myself . Another party. Great.

"Hey, in the morning, can I get a ride over to Princess Hilola's palace?" I asked as I stepped out of the jeep.

Cassandra's face went solemn, maybe for the first time since I'd met her. "I'm sorry to be the one to tell you, Kelley. That whole island went up in flames when the volcano erupted. The volcanic eruption tripped a sort of back door tunnel and allowed the lava to travel from the main volcano to some exit on the other island. It's the only reason why the fairgrounds aren't covered in molten magma right now."

I was caught off guard by this news. "Oh…Wow. Ok. So the volcano is real. You ever wonder how we were able to have a party in that very same volcano nearly a year ago?"

Cassandra shrugged, "I don't think about it all to be honest. I learned very early on to allow this place to not make sense. It keeps me sane."

"Ha," I nodded. "Smart."

"Well, I'm going to go back to Paul. Are you going to be ok, Kelley?" She asked, concerned.

I shrugged and tried to seem cool. "Yeah. I'm fine. Just going to drink the pain away." I managed a grin.

Cassandra grinned. "Ok, party boy. See you in a bit, yeah!" And she was back off down the road.

I made my way up to the bungalow and entered the party. The atmosphere was a celebratory one. Many of the partygoers I'd seen while they were working; servers, cashiers, attraction attendants. Everyone was dressed nicely and looked like they didn't have a care in the world, and maybe they didn't. I walked through the party looking for people I knew and couldn't find anyone. I looked for my old roommates, and I even found myself looking for Khamarri and the gang of "cool kids" I had spent the entire summer with, but I guess this party couldn't afford them. I was surrounded by nameless faces. People who came to the island with their own goals and aspirations. People who asked for my life in the name of the island and celebrated Princess Hilola's sacrifice. I wasn't in the partying mood. Like, at all. I made my way to the edge of the crowd where I found a small corner room with a couch big enough for me to curl up on. The continuous thumping of the music and the roaring ocean echoing through the open window kept me from my thoughts, and before I knew it, I'd woken to the sunrise dancing over me.

Disoriented, I got up and washed my face in the bathroom sink before exiting the bedroom. Outside some people were strung out on the floor, asleep. There was a bit of laughter and I heard a familiar accent coming from the balcony. I walked towards the sound, careful not to step on a glass of wine or a sleeping body.

My heart nearly melted through my ribcage when I saw my roommates all together on the balcony. They were gathered around a pot of coffee, cracking jokes and enjoying each other's company. I sat back and watched them interact with one another for a moment, and I thought about all the moments I'd missed out on. All the inside jokes. All the fights and good times I didn't get to see. When they noticed me in the doorway, the way they all turned and smiled at me, I had thought for a split second that maybe I hadn't woken up off the couch just yet.

"Well there goes the neighborhood. Kelley is conscious." Keith joked. He got up and hugged me. Slowly but surely they all did. César and Fausto enveloped me in a big group hug.

"So good to see you, meu amigo." Fausto nodded, pouring me a cup of coffee.

"How long have you all been here?" I sat beside them and accepted my cup of coffee with a nod. A goofy grin that I couldn't shake spread across my face. "You guys should've woken me up. I wanna hang."

"We agreed to let you rest." Edvin shifted in his seat. He was wearing his Paradise Parks and Resort chef uniform.

"They agreed. I wanted to wake you up as soon as your luggage arrived this morning." Paulie gushed.

"Oh yeah, this morning three town cars rolled up and three soldiers in Regina Hunama's regalia came to the front door carrying all your stuff." Paulie motioned into the house. "I left it by the door."

"My luggage?" I asked, perplexed.

I turned around and recognized my backpack and leather duffle, but beside it was a white Paradise Parks & Resort duffle bag and a bright red, smaller backpack. Those two pieces I didn't recognize at all, and though I wasn't going to outwardly say that, I couldn't help but furrow my brow. I thought it was best to change the subject.

"Why does your living room look like that, Paulie? What did you put in the punch, man?" I asked, accusingly, with a smirk on my face. Everyone laughed.

"Well, I couldn't just let a bunch of drunk people wander into the jungle after a flamingo tiger attack now, could I?" He shrugged.

"Flamingo tigers. Que besteira." César scoffed. "You've been bugging around all year about these beasts and I have yet to see one. ¿E aí, Paolo?"

"They're real!" Paulie whined, and suddenly he became the nervous butterball of a guy I met on the first day. "Not, besteira at all, Ceez!"

"Yeah, yeah, yeah." César folded his arms.

"So what was it like?" Keith spoke up. "Living with Princess Hilola. What was the whole experience like, and more importantly, was it worth it?"

I looked out over the balcony at the jungle, like I had done so many times at the tea haus. My friends, my real friends, waited patiently for me to answer.

"It was…very cool," I started, thoughtfully. "I learned a lot. It wasn't easy by any means. Yes, there was a sort of glitz and polish to it. But there were many days when I felt used, and disconnected, and there were days when I thought that none of it was real. Still not entirely sure if it was real. But I learned a lot. I guess I won't know if it was worth it, but still…I wish we'd done this more. I missed you guys."

"We missed you too." Keith patted my knee.

Edvin swirled his coffee a bit in his hand. "Do you think she's really gone?"

"I don't know. And you know what…" I shrugged and let out a sigh, "I don't really care."

I sipped my coffee with a cool grin as they all stared on, waiting for me to break.

"Well well," Fausto said with zest.

"Ok, Kelley." Edvin nodded back with the smallest of smiles. "Well I have to go back to work in a bit."

"Yeah, I have to meet Cassandra for lunch and then we're going to video call with her mom afterwards," Paulie said, finishing up his coffee.

"Really?" César asked, disgusted.

"What?" Paulie shrugged, clueless.

"You're in it thick, bruv," Keith joked. César couldn't stop shaking his head. "Anyways, the twins and I have to go finish packing. We leave tomorrow."

They were all getting up to leave and I found myself with nothing to do and nowhere to go. I didn't want this to end, but it was ending. Then I heard a noise in the distance. A horn echoing off in the air from the nearby ocean shore.

"Guys, I think I'm going to go ahead and leave today." I heard myself say before I even fully thought it through.

My roommates stopped in their tracks, and just looked at me.

"Why?" Paulie asked. "You don't have to. Kelley, you are more than welcome to stay here as long as you like."

"Thanks, Paulie." I stood and dusted myself off. "I feel it, though. It's hard to explain. There's just…nothing more. This, being with you guys, is the perfect ending."

Keith put out his hand. "You sure, mate?"

I took Keith's hand with a smile. The tightness in my throat prevented me from putting my feelings into words, so a nod was all I could muster.

"Dope." Keith nodded back at me. "Then let's get you there."

"I'll get the jeep!" Paulie darted into the house to put on his shoes.

Edvin stretched. "Welp. It was such a pleasure, Kelley…"

"We're ALL going, idiota." Fausto pushed Edvin aside as he walked past. Edvin let out the smallest groan.

We were all standing outside on the curb waiting.

"I forgot that Cassandra took the jeep this morning. Sorry." Paulie said sheepishly.

I adjusted the straps on my backpack while Paulie held the duffle bags. César wore the red pack and it clinked a bit while he played hacky sack with Fausto. Paulie checked his watch.

"Sorry it's taking so long," he apologized again. "Which dock are you being picked up from?"

"It's no problem," I replied, staring at a gigantic butterfly waft by on massive lime green wings. "I was hoping to catch the boat that takes the people who've been sent home back to the airport. The small red boat."

"I know that boat!" Paulie lit up. "That's right down the hill and down the beach! I run past there sometimes." He put the duffel bag strap over his chest and bent down to tighten his shoelaces.

"Well, um, then we won't be too late when the car gets here." Edvin stammered as we watched Paulie rush through a few basic leg stretches.

"The boat will be GONE by then! Let's go!" Paulie yelled cheerfully before running down the hill. There was a beat before Keith sprinted behind him, followed by César and Fausto, then myself and lastly Edvin.

We were off, sprinting down the hillside of the jungle, dodging roots that had broken through the asphalt and catching morning mists of dew in our faces.

"This way!" Paulie would yell cheerfully on occasion, leading the way.

At some point, César and Fausto started chanting futbol songs and joking with one another in Portuguese, which made us all laugh.

"Tortoise!!" Paulie yelled as he jumped hurdle-style over the giant moss-covered tortoise eating something in the road. I watched as Keith followed suit and jumped over it, followed by Fausto, then César, who front flipped over it. This granted a cheer from the gang. Feeling the peer pressure, I was able to perform a one-handed handstand off the shell and over the tortoise. Proud of myself, I stopped to bow gracefully as everyone applauded. We all stopped to watch Edvin, who merely ran around the tortoise.

"Long live Sweden!" he shouted desperately as we all burst into laughter, and back into a sprint.

I tried my best to stay in the moment and enjoy this with my roommates, but I couldn't ignore how much this reminded me of the mornings I ran with Moncyra and Tegra and Farrah. It felt like I'd been dreaming another life and had finally woken up to the real one, which could be just as good, if not better.

By the time we reached the dock, the boat was just leaving. I had just enough time to jump onboard. Paulie and César threw my bags onto the boat as it was pulling away.

I grabbed the duffles and red backpack away from the boat edge and let out a massive sigh of relief. I wiped my forehead and looked up to see my friends on the dock, all waving goodbye. It then occurred to me that we were so focused on getting me on the departing boat, that we never gave our proper goodbyes. I wanted so badly to jump off, but I was already several feet out at sea. I could plainly see the tears streaming down their faces as they waved. My own eyes were now burning as they filled up with tears, but I didn't cry. I was all cried out. The moment my friends were too far to see, I wiped my face and gazed up at the island itself. It looked like an enormous green anthill, or an enormous tree stump that had taken its roots in the ocean. I still felt the buzz of life within me, even as I turned away and looked forward toward whatever awaited next.

DAY - 32? - BOWVIOLET SPACE SHUTTLE - DAY 1? ON EARTH

Rebecca woke up in her sleeping chamber to the faint sound of a persistent dinging. After a moment it finally clicked that the dinging meant a breach in the space shuttle. Startled, she rose out of bed and grabbed her taser drill before heading to secure the control room.

When she arrived at the command station and checked the vitals on the screen, she saw that everything was stable. The breach came from an open door from the back end of the ship to the outside.

Rebecca spoke into the intercom. "Samuel, explain to me why there's a breach on the tail end of the shuttle."

She waited a moment for a response, and after nothing but silence, she called again.

"Samuel, do you copy?"

Still nothing. Rebecca tightened her grip around her taser drill.

"The hell is going on here?" She whispered to herself as she cautiously made her way through the hall towards the back of the ship.

When she arrived at the back door of the shuttle, she found it ajar with the exit ramp down and set firmly into the dark dirt. She shooed away a large blue king crab trying to board her ship before exiting herself, following the two pairs of footsteps in the ground.

Admittedly she was having a difficult time following the footsteps due to the constant distraction of her surroundings. The dark brown dusty soil contrasting against the heavy blueness of the sky. Gusts of massive and magnificent white clouds sailed over her head and gave her goosebumps. She heard the roaring of the ocean, but she had no clue where the sound was coming from as she clung to the footprints in the soil and hoped that they were ok.

After walking for what felt like hours, she scaled a mossy dune and there they were. Samuel was sitting cross-legged in the dirt facing the ocean. Beside him was a travel pack from the shuttle, her grandfather's clothes, and a small red backpack.

"Samuel, your insubordination is going to cost you severely for the duration of this mission!" Rebecca boomed as she stomped down the dunes towards him. "What the hell, man?"

"Have you ever seen anything so amazing?" Samuel asked with serenity. His eyes were glued to the horizon, where the sky and the ocean were indistinguishable.

Rebecca surveyed the horizon. It was beautiful, the way the murky turquoise waves rolled in and you washed up on shore. She paused as a passing seagull stopped to hover over them, study them, before sailing off down the shore. She sat down in the sand beside Samuel, tucking her knees close to her chest.

"Where's my great grandfather, Sammi?" She asked, exhausted.

Samuel nodded. "He's in the ocean. He made a B-Line directly for the ocean the moment he opened the shuttle door. By the time I'd caught up with him, he was already in his boxers, braving the sea. It's 15 celsius. I've checked. But he's out there."

Rebecca scanned the horizon again, searching for him, and saw nothing. Just waves flitting across the surface. A panic started to trickle into her breathing, when some distance out at sea, a figure rose gracefully like a buoy once submerged and finally set free. She watched with relief as her great grandfather ran water into his hands and washed it over his face and thin wiry gray hair. He looked over at them and swayed his arms widely. Rebecca waved back.

"You guys have got to join me!" He yelled. His voice boomed over the sound of the wind and the roar of the waves. Rebecca had never heard him so clear or seen him so energetic. "It's heaven!"

Samuel looked up at Rebecca. "Ever since we landed your great grandfather has been… different. His eyes-"

"Your insubordination will cost you as well!" Rebecca yelled to her great grandfather, knowing very well he couldn't hear her. She leaned over and grabbed a canister of water from the travel bag.

"Is that red backpack yours?" She asked casually.

Samuel shook his head. "It's his."

"No it's not." Rebecca said. "I packed and unpacked his luggage for this trip. I've never seen this bag before in my life, let alone on this shuttle."

Rebecca took a closer look at the backpack; it was weathered and ripped in places, and the red in the nylon fabric had faded into a dark pink in places. There was a small blue, yellow and green yarn woven ball in the mesh pocket on the side.

She hesitated for a moment, then decided to take the ball out. It was soft and filled with small seeds or rocks. It was a hacky sack.

She remembered the red bag at the end of Kelley's story.

She sat up and unzipped the backpack and discovered a trove of trinkets and precious memorabilia:

A plush velvet teapot cozy adorned with gold and orange tiger lily flowers, an old wrinkled visitor's map of Paradise Parks and Resort, and a small wooden tiki figure with it's hand outstretched, welcomingly.

"Oh, umm, there was a transmission received from Home Base. It's Monclair." Samuel tossed in her direction as he watched the waves. Rebecca continued to look through the backpack.

A chunk of ruby red quartz stone.

A lemon. An actual whole fresh lemon. It was shiny, unbruised, and in perfect shape.

"Oh my God." Rebecca squeezed the lemon slightly and put it to her nose.

"Wow." She gasped. "Sammi, smell this."

"What is it?" He asked, cautiously taking the fruit. He put it to his nose and his eyes widened. "Oh my."

"Oh my…" Rebecca sat there, mouth ajar. She pulled out a photo of six boys at the beach, huddled together smiling and making faces for the camera. They were attractive, happy and youthful. One of the boys had copper hair and smiled in a way that squished his nose slightly. She quickly wiped a tear from her cheek as she continued to gaze down at her 20 year old great grandfather.

"Uuurrghhh!!!!" Samuel growled and arched back.

Not missing a beat, Rebecca tuck'n'rolled away while simultaneously reaching for the taser drill.

"What is it?!!?" she shrieked.

Samuel's face was twisted and grimacing. In his palm was the lemon, now with a huge chunk taken out of it.

"That's so gross!" he snarled through pursed lips.

"Gimme that. No one asked you to bite it. Serves you right."

Rebecca rolled her eyes and put her weapon back in it's holster. She grabbed the lemon and studied the fleshy pulp insides. They glimmered and sparkled in the sun. Rebecca then put the fruit to her lips and took a sizable bite of it.

It was the sweetest, most refreshing thing she'd ever tasted.

"This is it!" Kelley yelled from the ocean. He was facing the sun with his hands outstretched in the air. Rebecca noticed the intricate scarring on his back. She couldn't make out the shape of it from a distance, but it spanned over his entire back. It looked familiar. "This is the beginning!"

Suddenly she felt a tingle in her hand. She tried to shake it off but it only intensified. She switched the lemon to her other hand and examined her palm, only to have the intense tingle appeared on her other hand as well. That's when, cupping the lemon in both hands, she realized that the lemon itself was vibrating. It was twitching in her hands, barely unable to contain whatever energy it contained.

"Kelley!" Rebecca yelled, arms outstretched, unsure what to do with an unstable lemon.

"This is where it all starts!" Kelley yelled emerging from the ocean, walking slowly towards them. Rebecca looked up from the lemon at her great grandfather, and gasped.

"This is just the beginning."

End of Log.